forever FOUR

• stories from New York •

GROSSET & DUNLAP
Published by the Penguin Group
Penguin Group (USA) Inc., 375 Hudson Street,
New York, New York 10014, USA
Penguin Group (Canada), 90 Eglinton Avenue East, Suite 700,
Toronto, Ontario M4P 2Y3, Canada
(a division of Pearson Penguin Canada Inc.)
Penguin Books Ltd., 80 Strand, London WC2R 0RL, England
Penguin Group Ireland, 25 St. Stephen's Green, Dublin 2, Ireland
(a division of Penguin Books Ltd.)
Penguin Group (Australia), 250 Camberwell Road, Camberwell,
Victoria 3124, Australia
(a division of Pearson Australia Group Pty. Ltd.)
Penguin Books India Pvt. Ltd., 11 Community Centre,
Panchsheel Park, New Delhi—110 017, India
Penguin Group (NZ), 67 Apollo Drive, Rosedale,
Auckland 0632, New Zealand
(a division of Pearson New Zealand Ltd.)
Penguin Books (South Africa) (Pty.) Ltd., 24 Sturdee Avenue,
Rosebank, Johannesburg 2196, South Africa

Penguin Books Ltd., Registered Offices:
80 Strand, London WC2R 0RL, England

Text copyright © 2012 by Elizabeth Cody Kimmel. Illustrations copyright
© 2012 by Penguin Group (USA) Inc. All rights reserved. Published by
Grosset & Dunlap, a division of Penguin Young Readers Group,
345 Hudson Street, New York, New York 10014. GROSSET & DUNLAP
is a trademark of Penguin Group (USA) Inc. Printed in the U.S.A.

Library of Congress Cataloging-in-Publication Data is available.

ISBN 978-0-448-45550-1 (pbk)   10 9 8 7 6 5 4 3 2 1
ISBN 978-0-448-46186-1 (hc)   10 9 8 7 6 5 4 3 2 1

forever FOUR

· stories from New York ·

by Elizabeth Cody Kimmel
Grosset & Dunlap
An Imprint of Penguin Group (USA) Inc.

For my fellow writer, Helena Smith—ECK

· chapter ·

1

I had one hand on the seat belt release as my mother pulled into the train station parking lot. I caught sight of my best friend standing on the platform. With her cranberry-colored hair in its neat signature bob and her high-tuned vintage fashion sense, Ivy Scanlon was hard to miss. Miko Suzuki stood next to her, checking her watch and peering up the track. A bolt of excitement shot through me. This was really happening! I was going on a three-day trip to New York City with my friends!

"Here we are," Mom said, giving me one of her careful looks. "I still can't get over it—an all-expenses-paid trip to visit *City Nation* magazine. What an opportunity! And you've only been working on *4 Girls* for what, three months?"

I nodded. "This one will be our third issue," I said.

"It seems like it was just a few weeks ago that the

four of you were pulling an all-nighter to get the first issue ready for the printer," my mother said, shaking her head and smiling.

"Well, Ivy came up with this great idea. We're going to make this one a web issue! All online, with video and everything. We won't need to worry about sending it to the printer."

"That is a great idea," my mother said, opening the car door. "I guess Ivy inherited her mother's publishing savvy."

"She definitely did," I said, stepping out of the car and into the chilly fall morning air. "Good thing for us, too!"

"Oh, there's Ivy's mom," my mother said. "I want to make sure she has my cell number. She's going to have her hands full, supervising the four of you and getting her own project for *City Nation* done. Who did you say she's interviewing again?"

"She still hasn't told us! It's a big secret!" I pulled my suitcase out of the backseat. "*City Nation* covers so much—fashion, current events, entertainment. All we know is it's for the cover article, and Mrs. Scanlon has arranged for us to watch the photo shoot and to each ask the person one question for *4 Girls*. But we may not know who it is until the very last minute."

"So it could be absolutely anybody," she said.

"Anybody!" I agreed. My brain was rattling,

wondering who it would be. A politician? A rock star? A famous actor? And how would we prepare our questions when we didn't know who we'd be talking to? The suspense was already killing me.

"Paulina!"

"*IIIIveeeee!*" I yelled back at my best friend, waving wildly with one hand and dragging my suitcase on its little wheels with the other as I walked up the ramp to the platform. She looked as excited as I felt. Even though she had lived in the city for years before moving upstate and had been in the *City Nation* office where her mom worked plenty of times, this trip was about US going together to find our own stories to tell our readers. Seeing Ivy's familiar face, her pale blue eyes flashing, I could hardly believe my good luck. Not only was I going to see New York City, I got to do it with my best friend and with Miko and Tally Janeway, the third and fourth founders and publishers of *4 Girls*, the magazine we published for the students—mainly the girls—of Bixby Middle School.

"Oh my gosh, Paulie, your suitcase is huge!" Miko exclaimed.

As usual, Miko looked like a team of stylists had spent an hour with her. She wore skinny jeans and high boots, and she had a purple scarf wrapped several times around her neck over a tailored jacket. Her long, glossy black hair hung perfectly around her face.

"*My* suitcase is huge?" I asked, laughing and pointing at the enormous red thing on wheels by Miko's feet. "What's that thing?"

"Well, this is the suitcase my mother made me bring," Miko said a little sheepishly. "She crammed all kinds of stuff in there that I know I don't need—a Windbreaker, rain boots, a down jacket. Like I'd wear any of that in New York City!"

"You're dressed perfectly for the city," Ivy told her. "That scarf is gorgeous."

I looked down at my own less than exciting jeans and tweed coat. I had more or less inherited my mom's taste for sensible clothes, though Ivy occasionally dragged me to the mall to help me find something supercute.

"There you are, Paulina. Are you all ready to go?" Mrs. Scanlon asked me.

I smiled at Ivy's mother. "I can't wait to get on the train! I tried to think of everything I'd need," I said. "But I have a feeling there might be a surprise or two that I'm not prepared for."

"Oh, you can count on that at *City Nation*," she told me, laughing. Then she turned to my mother, who had her cell phone out so she could double-check all the contact numbers.

"We have things scheduled at *City Nation* through Wednesday," Mrs. Scanlon was saying. "And I thought it would be nice if the girls could spend a few hours after that taking in some of the sights. Is it still okay with you if Paulina gets back Wednesday evening?"

"Oh yes, that's fine. I'd love for her to see the big city," my mother said. "Paulina's aunts will be helping me cook, and Kevin can pitch in, too."

Ivy and I exchanged a knowing look. My little brother was not likely to be much help in the kitchen or doing anything else Thanksgiving related. His expertise lay more in sci-fi trivia and karate moves.

"Your mom looks amazing," Miko murmured to Ivy as my mother and Mrs. Scanlon continued chatting. "That coat is gorgeous. I can't believe she's taking us all with her when she's got this big celebrity interview to run. She is extremely cool."

"That's sweet," Ivy said, looking as pleased as if Miko had given her the compliment.

Mrs. Scanlon was an older version of Ivy herself. They had the same delicate features and pale blue eyes. And wearing a crisp tailored suit and Jimmy Choo heels, Miko was right. Mrs. Scanlon did look amazing.

"Do you want me to wait with you until the train gets here?" my mom asked, smoothing my hair off my forehead.

"It's okay," I told her. "I know you need to go pick

Kevin up from his sleepover. I'll be fine, Mom."

My mom nodded. "I know that, honey. Give me a hug."

Normally I would find a public display of mother/daughter affection extremely embarrassing. But *normally* I was not leaving for New York City! I gave her a nice long hug, with an extra squeeze as a thank-you for letting me go.

"You're going to have the time of your life, sweetheart," she whispered. "Call me tonight once you're all settled."

"I will," I assured her. Then I watched her walk away, throwing glances over her shoulder and waving all the way to her car.

"Is that clock right?" Miko asked, pointing at a digital display near one end of the platform. "Because if it is, the train is going to be here in three minutes."

"Cool!" I said. Then I suddenly realized what Miko meant and exchanged a worried look with Ivy.

"She'll make it," I said with more confidence than I felt.

"Tally Janeway has never been on time for a thing in her life," Ivy corrected me. She looked up and down the length of the platform like Tally might be hiding somewhere, playing a joke on us.

What Ivy said was true. Tally was one of the most scattered, disorganized people I had ever met. The girl was a genius onstage but tended to be surrounded by drama offstage, too.

"I'm calling her cell," Miko said, already dialing her phone. She listened for a moment, then shook her head.

"Tally still isn't here?" Mrs. Scanlon asked.

"Miko's calling her cell phone," Ivy told her mother as she turned to watch Miko hopefully. But Miko shook her head again and snapped her phone closed.

"It went straight to voice mail," she said.

"She probably forgot to turn it on," Ivy said, smacking her forehead.

"What do we do?" I asked anxiously.

"There's nothing *we* can do," Ivy said. "Is there, Mom?"

Mrs. Scanlon checked the time on the station's display again.

"I'm afraid that unless she gets here in the next minute she will miss the train," Mrs. Scanlon said. "Unless the train is late, too."

But as we all looked at the display, which read TRAIN STATUS—ON TIME, my stomach clenched. Tally wasn't just going to miss the train; she would miss our big trip AND our chance to make *4 Girls* even bigger than the four of us.

"We should have realized this might happen. One of us should have picked Tally up," Ivy said with a groan.

"Tally's the one who's always late for stuff, not her parents," I pointed out. "Her mom seems pretty reliable."

"I should have insisted she let us come pick her up," Ivy said again, and I wondered if she even heard me.

"Sweetie, coordinating the drop-offs at the train station was my responsibility," Mrs. Scanlon said. "It's not your fault. Don't worry about it."

Miko tried Tally's cell again, then I tried it on my phone, too.

"I hear something," Ivy said. "I think it's coming."

Ivy was right. The train was coming, and Tally was nowhere in sight.

I held on tightly to the handle of my suitcase as the train squealed to a halt. As the doors slid open, I heard the sound of a car horn blaring in quick successive bursts. I turned around and saw a green minivan careening into the parking lot.

"That might be her!" I exclaimed excitedly, pointing. I felt a hand push firmly on my back.

"You need to get on the train, girls," Mrs. Scanlon said. "If that is Tally, she's going to have to run for it, and I can't risk any of you being left on the platform."

I shot one last agonized glance toward the parking lot, then got onto the train behind Ivy and Miko. My heart was pounding.

The aisles were narrow, and I had trouble with my

suitcase, which kept getting caught on the armrests of the seats. Up ahead, Ivy had found a four-seater and was getting herself settled. When Miko reached the seats, she turned around and looked at me.

"Did Tally make it?" Miko asked.

"I don't know," I said. I looked behind me, hoping to see her there. But it was just a line of people looking for seats. Not a curly blond lock or bubbly personality to be found.

We took turns hoisting our suitcases up onto the luggage rack. The train lurched as we began to move, and I dropped into the seat beside Ivy.

That was it then. Tally hadn't made it.

The three of us sat in silence as the train pulled out of the station.

"Let's google train and bus schedules to see what her options are to still get into the city," Ivy suggested. "I don't know if I feel bad for Tally or if I want to kill her!"

That was a good idea. Googling schedules, that is—not killing Tally.

"But how will we tell her if she's not answering her phone?" I asked.

Miko and Ivy looked at me like I'd just asked them to name all the state capitals in fifty seconds or less. Finally, Miko said, "Let's just see what the choices are. Then we can go from there."

I fiddled with my phone, waiting for it to connect to the Internet. I stared at the trees outside the window, which were becoming blurs as we picked up speed. Suddenly, the door to our car crashed open, followed by a flurry of *oomph*s and *I'm sorry*s.

Miko leaned into the aisle and looked for the cause of all the commotion. In my spot by the window, I couldn't see what was going on.

"What is it?" I asked.

Miko sat back in her seat and gave me a huge grin.

"Guess," she said.

I stood up, almost slamming my head into the luggage rack.

Tally Janeway was coming down the aisle. She looked like she'd just been tossed out of a tornado. Her coat was misbuttoned, her long, curly blond hair was shooting out in every direction, and she had a piece of brown packing tape stuck to her arm. She was looking in every seat for us and turning around to talk to Mrs. Scanlon at the same time.

"Sorry," Tally said each time she looked into a seat and didn't find us. "Sorry. So sorry."

"Tally!" I yelled, way louder than I meant to.

When Tally saw me, she rushed forward down the aisle to our four-seater, collapsing in a heap in the empty spot.

"Hey, y'all!" She took a deep breath, trying to get some air into her lungs.

"Is that all you have to say? Tally, you almost gave me a heart attack!" Ivy said.

"As you can see, we have our Tally after all. Settle in, girls. We have a three-hour trip ahead of us," Mrs. Scanlon said, smiling warmly and shaking her head as she settled into the seat behind us.

"We didn't think you'd make it," Miko said.

"The conductor saw me runnin', and I was hollerin' for all I was worth," Tally explained. "And he took pity on me and held the door!"

"We were supposed to meet at the train station ten minutes early," Ivy said.

"You told me fifteen," Tally said.

"Yep, and it still didn't help," Ivy said.

"Oh, but I was so organized, you wouldn't believe it! I was all packed last night, and we left my house at the exact minute we planned to. Only we got halfway to the station, and I realized I'd forgotten my cell phone, and I knew y'all would be mad because Ivy's mom made us all promise to have them! So we went back for it, but I had a little trouble finding it because I distinctly remember putting it down next to the bread box when I was making toast, but for some reason it ended up in the freezer, where I never even would have looked, except the bread box is white and so is ice, well, not white but frosty, and—"

I stopped the stream of words by leaning forward and giving Tally a hug.

"I am so, so, SO glad you made it!" I told her. "As soon as I thought you really weren't going to make it, I realized how much fun we'd all miss without you."

Tally beamed at me. Her face was bright red—she must have been running like lightning from the parking lot.

"Well, the important thing is you made it," Miko said. "And at least you tried to be organized. I was still cramming stuff in my suitcase until the last minute this morning."

"Wait a minute," Ivy said suddenly. "Tally . . . where *is* your suitcase?"

Tally's mouth dropped open into a silent O.

"You forgot your suitcase?" Miko asked, astonished.

Tally looked genuinely mystified.

"Uh-oh," she said.

There was a long silence while all four of us tried to figure out what we would do about the latest Tally Incident. Then, suddenly, the whole thing struck me as hilarious. I began to laugh, silently at first, then in a stream of giggles. Tally joined in while Miko and Ivy watched the two of us and shook their heads.

"How could anyone forget their suitcase?" Miko asked.

Tally shrugged and made a twirling motion by her ear.

She is nuts, I thought. But she was also incredibly fun. Tally had a way of attracting disaster, but she rarely got down about it. Her sunny view on things and her wild excitement about almost everything was contagious. When I was with her, I felt like I was in a crazy but hilarious movie.

"So, guys, I have this month's *City Nation*," I said, pulling the magazine out of my bag. "Have you seen it? I thought maybe we could get some ideas about what to expect."

"Oh, I have!" Tally exclaimed. "The tribute to silent movie stars was *sooo* beautiful! If I were a silent movie star, I . . . I would . . ."

Even Tally did not seem to be able to process a version of herself that was silent.

"I think Paulina means the magazine as a whole," Ivy said. "Remember, we'll be working in a few different departments. Later today we're supposed to go to editorial and design meetings. Maybe we should split up and have two of us go to one and two of us go to the other, so we can cover more. Then tomorrow we're going to sit in on the final prep meeting for the cover photo shoot, then watch the shoot itself. That's when we'll get to ask the celebrity our questions. In the afternoon, we're going to watch

13

them make storyboards, and on Wednesday we'll check out some of the pictures from the shoot while they're laying out the article. Other than business and accounting, we're going to be seeing most of the major departments."

"I still don't see how we're supposed to come up with questions for the cover person when we have no idea who it is," Tally stated.

It was a good point, one I'd been asking myself a bunch of times.

"We're just going to have to be ready for anything," Ivy said. "And remember what my mom told us: Things go wrong just as often as not. So there's a possibility there won't be time for us to ask our questions at all. Or even that they'll switch to a different person for the cover. We're just going to have to play it by ear."

"That's right. Be ready for anything," I said, pulling my little video camera from my bag. "Starting now—time to record our first video entry for our web issue."

"Oh, great idea!" Ivy said. She turned around and hung over the back of her seat. "Mom, can you film us for a minute?"

"Sure," Mrs. Scanlon said, reaching over and taking the camera from me. "Why don't all four of you squish into the seat facing me."

Ivy and I piled on top of Miko and Tally.

"Ready? I'm recording," Mrs. Scanlon said.

Never shy about being on camera, Tally jumped right in.

"Hey, y'all! *4 Girls* here, heading into New York City to bring you an all-web edition of *4 Girls* from none other than *City Nation* magazine!"

Tally nudged me.

"We're going to spend the next few days seeing how things run at one of the most popular magazines out there," I said, holding up my copy.

"We're going to go behind the scenes in everything from design meetings to a photo shoot," Miko added. "So if you've got any questions, post them to our blog, and we'll try to answer them for you."

"We're going to post articles, photographs, and videos of everything we can," Ivy said. "And we're going to keep you updated on the question that's been keeping the four of us up at night—who is the mystery celebrity who'll be featured on the cover?"

"And what question should each of us ask him or her if we get the chance?" Tally asked. "Stay tuned to find out!"

"Okay, that was great," Mrs. Scanlon said. "You've created a sense of anticipation to keep your readers checking back."

"So . . . who IS the mystery celebrity?" I asked with a grin.

Mrs. Scanlon laughed. "For now, you're going to have to stick to your own advice and stay tuned," she told me.

As if we had a choice—the four of us had front-row seats to the show!

· chapter ·

2

When we got off the train in New York, my breath caught in my throat and my heart began to race. I was in awe of the massive expanse of Grand Central Terminal, its vaulted ceilings painted with constellations. The main room looked as big as a football field and was crowded with people moving one way or another and somehow managing not to collide. Mrs. Scanlon led us past a row of shops, including a bookstore, a coffee shop, and a chocolate store packed with customers. A brightly lit display of breads and cakes caught my eye, and a delicious smell stopped me in my tracks. Ivy ran into me with an "Oomph!" She looked at the storefront.

"Eli's," she said, grinning as I stared wide-eyed at an enormous stack of cupcakes. "Best bakery in the world."

I could believe that. The smell was intoxicating,

and I felt like I could stand there all morning just sniffing.

Mrs. Scanlon ushered us quickly through the crowds, and before taking us out the door and into the city for real, she gathered us around her.

"Okay, girls. The hotel is just a few blocks away from Grand Central, so we'll walk there," she said. "Everybody stay close to me. We'll go check in and drop our bags in our suite, then we'll go over to *City Nation*. Everybody ready?"

Tally gave a whoop and grabbed my arm. "I'm about to step foot in New York City for the first time!" she cried.

"Tal, you're already here. This *is* New York City," Ivy said, motioning all around us.

Tally shook her head. "I'm not there until we go through that door," she said.

"Well, let's not keep New York City waiting then," Mrs. Scanlon said, pushing the door open.

My senses were on overload the second I stepped outside. The sounds of cars and buses and horns and people's voices made me want to turn in every direction at once. There were a million smells—hot dogs and car exhaust and, as a beautifully dressed woman walked by, a whiff of perfume. The buildings around us were so tall, I felt like I'd shrunk down to two feet in size. There were streams of people on

18

the sidewalk, all of them moving quickly, in a hurry to get somewhere or see something. If we weren't sticking close to Ivy's mom, I could imagine running up and down every street. I wanted to see it all.

"Everybody keep an eye on Tally," Ivy said. She had already stopped to kneel on the sidewalk, saying she wanted to get as close to New York as she could, and we had almost walked off without her.

We walked single file on the sidewalk, making sure Tally stayed between Mrs. Scanlon and Ivy.

"Is it always this crowded?" I asked Ivy, amazed.

"Depends on the time of day," she told me. "This isn't even rush hour. But Thanksgiving week is a huge tourist time. You should see Rockefeller Center at Christmas when they've got the tree up. Now *that's* crowded!"

"Two more blocks," Mrs. Scanlon called over her shoulder.

"Where exactly are we going?" I asked Ivy.

"Well, this is Forty-Second Street," she said. "Our hotel is on the same street, but two blocks that way, just past Fifth Avenue. The city is divided into east and west by Fifth Avenue. So Grand Central is on East Forty-Second Street, and our hotel is on West Forty-Second."

I nodded, though I still didn't really understand. New York City was complicated.

We crossed a busy intersection when the walk sign flashed. "Watch out for the bike messengers," Ivy cautioned. "Sometimes they don't stop."

"Oh look!" Tally said, pointing excitedly.

"Tal, get across the street first, then gawk," Miko said sternly.

"But look at the lions!" Tally cried.

A huge, beautiful building that took up the entire block was on our left. A large staircase led up to the front doors, and it was flanked by massive stone lions.

"That's the main branch of the New York Public Library," Ivy explained. "And all the space behind it is Bryant Park. Our hotel is right at the end of this block."

"So we'll be near the Fashion District, right?" Miko asked. "This is amazing. I feel like I'm dreaming!"

"Me too," Tally agreed, trotting to keep up. Mrs. Scanlon was walking really fast. We followed her the length of the block to the next intersection, where Ivy pointed at a sign that said 6 AVENUE.

"If for some reason you ever get lost, just get yourself to Forty-Second and Sixth. That building with the red awning is our hotel," Mrs. Scanlon told us.

I could not imagine being able to find my way to the hotel if I got lost. The city seemed to stretch on forever in every direction. Each building seemed taller than the last, and every sidewalk more crammed with people.

Miko nudged me as we crossed the street. "Can you believe how casually she said that? 'If for some reason you get lost.' I would flip out!"

"Seriously," I agreed.

"This is it, everyone!" Mrs. Scanlon said, gesturing toward the building with the red awning. A white-haired man with bright blue eyes held the door open for us. His uniform made him look very elegant, and his name tag said "Mel."

"Hi, Mel. I'm Tally!" Tally announced as we walked through the door. "This is my first time in New York City!"

Mel smiled and tipped his hat. "Welcome to Manhattan, Tally," he said.

"Everybody with me?" Mrs. Scanlon said as we gathered in the lobby. "I'm just going to check us in and get our key. Ivy, have everyone wait together by the elevators, okay?"

The lobby was small but elegant. The walls were covered with black-and-white photographs of movie stars and other famous people. One end of the room had a long, shiny desk, and the other side had sleek red chairs and couches. The floors were a gleaming reddish marble and from the ceiling hung a crystal chandelier.

"Oh, it's like a little palace!" Tally exclaimed.

"Hey, look at that picture!" Miko exclaimed, pointing to a framed photo of an elegant, dark-haired woman wearing strings of pearls. "That's Coco Chanel. She was, like, the most famous designer in the world. Do you think that her picture hanging here means she might have stayed here once?"

"Oh, you should ask!" Tally said, admiring the picture. "Isn't she gorgeous? Maybe someone here even met her."

But before we could ask, Mrs. Scanlon was back. "Here we go," she said. "Suite 501. Let's get settled in quickly because we're going to have to head right back out again. Tally, the hotel is going to send up a courtesy bag for you with things like a toothbrush and a comb. I'm afraid they can't help you with clothes, though. You'll have to borrow from whomever is closest to your size. Miko, maybe?"

Tally nodded agreeably, but I noticed Miko looked less than thrilled.

"I can't believe we're actually here," I whispered to Ivy as we got into the elevator. "Your mom seems so calm."

"You should see her at the office," Ivy said. "It can get kind of crazy there, and the more it does, the calmer she gets. I wish I could learn to do that."

22

"Oh please. You're the calmest person I know," I told her.

To my left, Tally was singing "New York, New York," and Miko was trying to get her to stop.

"Yeah, not such a huge accomplishment to look like the calmest person in this group," Ivy said good-naturedly as our elevator reached the fifth floor with a *ping*.

"We're here!" Tally squealed.

"Tally, you cannot do this when we get to *City Nation*," Miko said as we followed Mrs. Scanlon out of the elevator. "You have to be quiet in an office." She gave me and Ivy a look that seemed to say, "Can Tally possibly be quiet *anywhere?*"

Suite 501 was right next to the elevator. Mrs. Scanlon slid the key through the slot and opened the door.

Tally burst into the room ahead of us, since she was the only one not weighed down by a suitcase. There was a very small central room with a television, couch, and a tiny kitchen area with a minifridge and microwave beneath two small windows.

"There are three bedrooms in the suite with two double beds each," Mrs. Scanlon told us. "You'll share two rooms between you, and I'll take the third."

"Want to share with me, Paulie?" Ivy asked me quickly.

"Yes!" I exclaimed. Then I saw Miko make a little face. She was superneat, and Tally was notoriously messy. But Tally threw her arms around Miko and squealed, "Roomie!" and Miko smiled.

"But seriously, you have to stop squealing," Miko said while hugging Tally back.

"Take fifteen minutes to put your things away and freshen up, but then we should really get going," Ivy's mom said, already texting someone on her phone in one hand and pulling her suitcase into her room with the other.

"Your mom can totally multitask," Miko said, looking impressed.

Ivy nodded. "We really better get moving if she wants us ready in fifteen minutes," she said.

Tally shot into the door closest to us, then shot out again.

"Oops! Bathroom!" she cried, darting into the next room. "Dibs on this one!" she yelled.

Miko made a face at me. "Do I really have to share with Tally?" she murmured. "She'll turn the place into a wreck."

"No, she won't," I told Miko cheerfully. "She forgot her suitcase, remember? What can she make a mess with?"

"She'll find a way," Miko mumbled, pulling her enormous suitcase into the room.

"Guess that room is ours then," Ivy said, and I followed her inside.

Our room was tiny but beautiful. Everything was supermodern, from the gleaming metal lamps to the sleek armchairs and the elegant little desk.

"We should just hang up the stuff that might get wrinkled," Ivy said. "And I need to fix my hair."

"I'm going to change into my black pants," I said, unzipping my suitcase and pulling the pants out.

"Oh, should I change, too? I don't think I like what I have on. And I should have brought my straightening iron. This piece by my ear keeps sticking out. I look ridiculous!"

I looked at Ivy, surprised. She rarely worried about her appearance. She had great taste in clothes and her sleek cranberry bob was always perfectly styled, never a hair out of place.

"Ivy, you look amazing, as usual," I reassured her. "You're the only one that's lived here and actually been to *City Nation*. You aren't nervous about being back, are you?"

Ivy was staring at her unopened suitcase. She suddenly seemed to hear my question and looked at me. "Why? Am I acting funny? And don't give me the nice answer. Give me the best friend answer."

"You're not acting funny at all," I said. "And you DO look amazing. But I am your best friend so . . .

25

you just seem like something might be bugging you."

Ivy sighed and sat down on the edge of the bed.

"No, you're right," she said. "Here's the thing. There's this girl we're probably going to see. Her name's Dakota. Her dad works at *City Nation,* too— he's the head of business operations. I've known her, like, forever, basically. And my mom told me that she's an intern this year, meaning she works there after school and during vacations."

"Oh," I said. "So we'll definitely see her. That's okay, right? It always helps to have a friend around."

But Ivy shook her head. "I said I've known her forever, but I wouldn't exactly call us friends. Ever since kindergarten, we've been ending up in the same stuff—karate class, skating camp, gymnastics. Dakota is insanely competitive, and everything was a race with her. Who got their black belt first, who could skate backward better, who could do the best vault. I know it sounds stupid, but it used to really upset me. Like there was nothing I couldn't do that she wasn't right there trying to do better. We both used to talk about interning at *City Nation* when we were old enough. But then we ended up moving, and now Dakota's an intern. And I never got to be one. I'm afraid she is going to gloat or something. Not that it really matters. I just kind of dread seeing her."

I sat next to Ivy and put my arm around her. "I'd

feel the same way," I said. "It's only for a few days, though, and you've got your *own* magazine to boast about! Maybe she'll be really intimidated by you now."

"And maybe she won't be," Ivy said. "But you're right. It's only a few days, and besides, we have totally different lives now." She jumped up and checked her reflection in the mirror, smoothing her hair and turning slightly to the side. "You really think I should wear this?" she asked.

I pulled on my black pants and stood next to Ivy in the mirror. "I do. Really," I told her.

A smile spread across Ivy's face as she turned to face me. "Then what are we waiting for? Let's go!"

• • • • • • •

The offices of *City Nation* were about six blocks from our hotel, in a part of New York Mrs. Scanlon kept calling Midtown. We walked down Sixth Avenue to get there, trying to stay together as a group while also avoiding bumping into the crowds of people, many of them carrying shopping bags, texting, or stopping to take pictures.

When we reached one street corner, Tally let out a huge scream. "Y'all! It's the Empire State Building!" she shouted, pointing up into the sky.

"The one and only," Mrs. Scanlon said, pausing to take a head count. "We should have some time later in the week to see some of the city. We can go up to the top of the Empire State Building if you'd like. But for now, here it is, guys. *City Nation*."

I stared up at the narrow, seemingly all-glass building. There was no sign outside, nothing to indicate what was inside. "I always imagined there'd be a huge sign over the door," I said to Ivy as we walked into the lobby.

"*City Nation* is big, but not that big," Ivy explained. "This is a forty-story building. The magazine has maybe three floors, but the rest are other companies. You have to sign in and get a pass to go anywhere."

Mrs. Scanlon was already talking to a woman at the security desk in front of the bank of elevators. We each had to be photographed and were given a badge with our name and picture to wear.

"Oh, one of my eyes is closed," Tally complained, examining her picture. "Will they let me have a do-over? It doesn't look like me."

"Tally, you're right here," Miko said. "It doesn't matter if the picture looks like you or not because it's stuck to the real you."

"Oh, I guess that makes sense," Tally admitted.

Miko noticed me looking at her and rolled her eyes, but at the same time she reached up and tucked the tag of Tally's jacket back inside her coat at the neck, then smoothed her scarf down.

It was funny. The more Miko complained about Tally, the more it became obvious to me that she was getting to really like her. When school had started in September, Miko, Tally, and I didn't know each other all that well, and Ivy had been the new girl at school. We'd been thrown into working together on *4 Girls* and had found a way to keep it friendly during the school-wide competition to determine who would win a year of funding for their project. But after we won the competition and got to keep publishing *4 Girls* together, we really became friends.

The elevator took us to the thirty-second floor, where we went through big glass doors to yet another lobby. This one did have a sign—a massive black rectangle with huge white letters saying CITY NATION. The young woman sitting behind the desk looked like a movie star—she had glossy, long hair that hung old-Hollywood style over one eye and bright red lipstick perfectly applied. She was dressed all in black, sitting up completely straight behind the desk. I got the feeling nobody got past her unannounced.

Mrs. Scanlon said something I couldn't hear, and the receptionist dialed the phone and said something even more quietly. That's when I noticed that the whole lobby felt as hushed as a library. I felt loud just standing there breathing.

But the silence was interrupted by the *clackety-clack*

of someone walking in high heels. The woman walking down the hallway seemed to project a force field of severity around her. She had jet-black hair that was cut bluntly near her jawline, one side hanging lower than the other, and a single stripe of silver hair. She was dressed entirely in light purple, from her elegantly tailored jacket to her lethal-looking stilettos. She wore a tiny telephone headset and was talking into it as she walked. It looked like she was talking to herself.

"Get it done," I heard her say. Then she reached up and touched a button on the headset as she reached the lobby.

"Karen, so glad you're here. We're behind on ten things that I need done before the advertising meeting next week, and you're the only one who's going to be able to get them all done right." Then she turned to us as though she were just realizing we were there. A wide smile spread across her face, and it terrified me a little to be under this woman's intense gaze. "Welcome, girls! I am Helvetica Grenier, the editor in chief of *City Nation* magazine."

Tally made a quiet little "hello" sound without actually speaking, and Miko looked like she was holding her breath. I smiled politely, trying not to look as nervous as I felt.

Even I had heard of Helvetica Grenier. You could

not read magazines, watch awards shows like the Oscars, or check out a TV show like *Hollywood Happening* without eventually seeing Helvetica interviewed or weighing in with an expert opinion. Her friends were all famous or rich, and most often both. As the editor in chief of *City Nation* magazine, she had the world at her feet, and her employees and people in the entertainment industry seemed to live in fear of disappointing her. I had heard she could be a tough boss and was extremely demanding, and that her opinion was the only thing that really mattered in the entertainment world. I had also heard one other thing about Helvetica Grenier: She always dressed all in one color, but the color was never the same from one day to the next.

"And these must be the famous four girls I've been hearing about," she said, looking us up and down. I was very glad I'd changed into my black dress pants instead of standing in front of Helvetica in blue jeans with frayed hems.

"Paulina Barbosa, Tally Janeway, Miko Suzuki, and you've met my daughter, Ivy Scanlon," Mrs. Scanlon said, giving each of us an encouraging smile as she introduced us.

"Welcome to all of you," Helvetica said again. "I had hoped to give you a tour myself, but I've just been told that my three o'clock has been moved to now, and I really need to jet. Karen, I have a few last-minute things I need to run by you," she added, drawing Ivy's mom slightly aside.

"I've never seen anyone wear all purple before," Tally whispered, looking awestruck.

"That's supposed to be her trademark look," I responded. "Always all one color. I read a whole article about it."

The receptionist cleared her throat, and all four of us turned to look at her. "Don't call it purple," she murmured. "Today's color is Caledonia Thistle."

"Caledonia Thistle," Tally murmured. "How absolutely dreamy."

"I'll have Constantia make the calls," Helvetica was saying. "Girls, I have to dash, but welcome to *City Nation*. Perhaps I'll see you shortly. We're very pleased to have such young and accomplished publishers here."

With that, she turned on her heel and began striding back up the hall, her heels echoing on the floor long after she'd disappeared. *How can anyone walk so fast in shoes like that?* I wondered.

· chapter ·
3

After Helvetica went off to her meeting, Mrs. Scanlon gestured for us to gather around her. "Okay, girls, here's the plan. I need to run up to editorial to check in with my team and go over a few quick items. Then I'll show you around the office a little, and we'll get you sitting in with some of the different departments. So for now, I'm going to introduce you to a few junior interns and let you hear from them about what it's like to work here."

Ivy caught my eye. "Dakota," she mouthed, and I nodded.

"What are interns?" Tally asked.

Mrs. Scanlon was already walking down the hall in the direction Helvetica had gone, and we scrambled to catch up.

"Well, Tally, they're people who need experience in the field. Being an intern is sort of like doing a training program. They have the opportunity to work for the magazine and learn the ropes of the business," she told us. "Some of them are college students, but *City Nation* also has a junior intern program for younger people. We have several interns about your age who come in after school and sometimes during their vacations."

"Oh, I want to be a *City Nation* intern!" Tally breathed.

"Tally, you could barely get yourself to one train," Miko scolded. "Imagine trying to get to an office every day at the same time."

"Every day at the same time?" Tally asked, looking genuinely surprised.

Miko laughed. "You better stick with acting," she suggested.

Mrs. Scanlon had led us down the hall past a huge, open area filled with cubicles. One wall was lined with offices. We took a turn down a smaller hallway, and she stopped outside a door.

"Everyone here?" she asked, checking her watch. "Oh goodness, I didn't realize how late it was. I really need to get upstairs. Let me quickly introduce you."

We followed her into a windowless room lined with filing cabinets. There were four desks set up in a square formation. Each desk had a computer, a phone, and piles of files and papers. A guy who didn't look much older than me sat at one desk. He had light brown hair and little round glasses, and he was squinting at the computer screen like his glasses weren't helping much.

"Whit!" exclaimed Ivy. "What are you doing here?"

The guy with the glasses looked at Ivy, blinked a few times, then stood up so fast his chair shot backward.

"Ivy! No way!" he exclaimed, coming around his desk to give Ivy a hug. "Since when are you back in town?"

"Since now!" she told him. "I e-mailed you I was coming, but it bounced back."

"New address. I just switched accounts," he explained. "Sorry about that."

Miko nudged me and raised her eyebrows in a questioning look. I shrugged. I had no idea who the guy was.

"Whit Clayton! Are you a junior intern this year?" asked Ivy's mother.

"Yep," Whit said, grinning at Mrs. Scanlon. "Mom said it would be good on my college applications, but I think she just wants someone to keep an eye on me after school."

"Whit's mother used to run our marketing department, before she left us to write novels. Please tell her I said hello, will you, Whit? I've got a meeting to get to, so I'm going to be rudely quick about this.

Whit and Dakota, meet Paulina, Tally, and Miko, of *4 Girls* magazine. Of course you both know Ivy—she can fill you in on the details. I'll be back as soon as I can."

Before we could even say good-bye, Mrs. Scanlon had hurried out the door. From what I'd seen so far, everyone seemed to be in a hurry at *City Nation*.

There was a momentary silence. That's when I noticed the girl by the filing cabinet, obviously Dakota, staring at us. She was tall and willowy, with long blond hair and piercing hazel eyes. Her gaze settled on Ivy, who was staring back at her.

"So you know Ivy?" I asked Whit. I couldn't wait to get Ivy alone to interrogate her about this guy. He was kind of adorable.

"Only since kindergarten," Whit said. "On the first day of school, she threw up in my backpack and we both got sent to the nurse's office."

"Um, excuse me," Ivy said, laughing. "You threw up in *my* bag."

"Are you still sticking to that story? I am going to find that nurse and have her settle this once and for all. You were the hurler and my bag was the hurlee!" Whit insisted.

"So you've been arguing about this ever since?" I asked.

"That's right," Whit said. "And we probably will for the rest of our lives."

Ivy looked a little embarrassed, but she smiled nonetheless. I glanced at Dakota, who was now scowling slightly. Even though it seemed like Dakota was the one who should have said hello, I was starting to feel rude not even acknowledging her.

"Were you in kindergarten with them, too, Dakota?" I asked.

"Yes, lucky me," she said. "All the way through sixth grade, until she moved out to the sticks. It's probably a good thing you did, Ivy. Seventh grade in the city is killer—though I've managed to stay on the honor roll."

"What? Bixby Middle School must be easy because it's not in Manhattan?" Ivy challenged.

Dakota shrugged. "You said it, not me. I mean, everything's less intense outside of the city. There can't be all that much to do there."

"Oh, there're tons of things to do! Actually, we publish our own magazine. It's called *4 Girls*. We're doing a special issue about *City Nation*!" Tally told her. "We're going to sit in on the cover shoot and interview him! Or her. We're not exactly sure who the cover person is yet."

"Yeah, I heard something about your little magazine," Dakota said, making quotes with her

37

fingers when she said *magazine*. "You call it *4 Girls*? It sounds like a Girl Scouts newsletter. You'd need something much more sophisticated if you wanted it to fly in Manhattan."

Tally's mouth dropped open, and Whit quickly jumped to his feet.

"Don't mind Dakota. She's just in a bad mood because she's been banned from the sample room for the day," he said. He shot her a look that seemed to say "You can live without new shoes for one day."

"The Louboutins are coming in, Whit," Dakota said. "It's not some random day."

"Are they being interviewed?" I asked, hoping to start getting a feel for what was going on at *City Nation* today.

"Louboutins are shoes, Paulina," Miko said. "And not just *any* shoes. They're like the Rolls-Royce of shoes."

"Exactly," Dakota said, walking over to a spare desk and sitting down behind it. She gave Miko an appraising look. "If I was there when they arrived, I'd be practically the first girl in New York to see their newest line! Sometimes you even get to try them on."

"Wow," Miko said. "You're really lucky to intern here. I'd do anything to see the new Louboutins before they come out."

"Oh well," Dakota said, tucking her hair behind her ear. "I always make sure I'm in with the right people, so I can see the really cool stuff."

"So what's it like working here?" Miko asked, pulling up a metal folding chair and sitting down near Dakota's desk. "I mean, I've heard the stories about how hard it is to get a job like this because everybody in the world wants to work here. And then how easy it is to get fired if you make the, uh . . . wrong person mad. Is all that stuff about Helvetica Grenier true? Like how she has this rare white tea flown in from India every week? Or that you're not supposed to get on the elevator if she's on it? Or that she has a full-time consultant whose only job is to choose what colors she's going to wear?"

Dakota rolled her own chair around the desk, then she swiveled until she was facing Miko.

"You wouldn't believe half of it," she said.

Tally grabbed an empty chair, plopped down in it, then shoved off with both feet so the chair glided several feet in Dakota's direction.

"What is the deal with the colors?" Tally asked. "I said Helvetica was wearing purple, and the receptionist practically had a cow."

"That wasn't purple. It was Caledonia Thistle," Dakota said automatically, not looking at Tally.

Miko laughed. "Okay, but how do you know that? For all anyone knows it could be called Pastoral Plum or Fountain of Fuchsia."

Dakota smiled. "Hah, that's good. So here's the thing with Helvetica's outfits. Every day she wears a new color—everybody knows that part. She comes in every morning at nine on the nose except for Tuesdays. By 9:01, everyone at the entire magazine has gotten an e-mail with the name of the color. That's when some people have to hide."

"Hide?" I asked, looking at Whit. "Why?"

"Until they know if they're wearing the same color," Whit said.

I looked back and forth between Whit and Dakota, confused.

"Just listen, I'm explaining it," Dakota said impatiently. "Okay, so say Helvetica comes in today in Caledonia Thistle, which is basically like light purple—lavender maybe. Anybody who's wearing that color or something she might consider too close to that color has to take it off. Helvetica's color of the day is *hers*, and nobody else is allowed to wear it."

"Take it off?" Miko asked. "What if it's, like, a shirt or something?"

Dakota laughed. "Then that person has problems. If they're lucky, they might be able to borrow something from the sample room to wear. Otherwise, they've got to rush home or at the very least go over to Bloomingdale's or something. People get insane over the color of the day."

"But it gets even more complicated than that," Whit added. "Sometimes people don't think they're wearing the same color as Helvetica, but she decides they are."

"Whit, remember that one time? See, there was this marketing meeting last month in the morning," Dakota said. "And the color of the day turned out to be Umbrian Sepia, which is basically kind of a reddish brown. So Helvetica walks into the conference room, and there's this junior rep at the table wearing this jacket that was sort of rust colored."

"I thought it was more of a deep pumpkin," Whit said.

"No, it wasn't," Dakota said. "It was closer to russet, actually, didn't you think?"

"Baked yam," Whit suggested, and Dakota giggled, then shot Ivy a look. I couldn't be sure, but it seemed as if she was trying to say "See how well Whit and I get along?" I had only known Dakota a few minutes, and I could already see what Ivy meant about how competitive she was.

"Anyway," Dakota continued, "whatever color it was, Helvetica decided it belonged in the Umbrian Sepia family. So she just stood there, glaring at this girl who thought she was wearing orange and had no idea what the problem was."

Whit was laughing, too. "And apparently the girl thought Helvetica was waiting for someone to take her coat," Whit added. "So she gets up and tries to sort of help her out of this billion-dollar Italian-leather thing that's the perfect shade of Umbrian Sepia, and Helvetica shouts . . . what was it again, Dakota?"

"'Unhand that jacket!'" Dakota said, in what I realized was an extremely good imitation of the editor's voice.

"Yeah, that's it!" Whit agreed. "And the girl, who's already totally terrified of Helvetica—because everyone is, because she's *Helvetica*—just burst into tears, and finally one of the design guys pulled her outside and explained what the problem was."

"He sent her home to change, and she never came back," Dakota added. "Nobody ever saw her again."

"She died?" Tally asked a little breathlessly.

Dakota shot her an impatient look. "Um, no. She quit."

"Well, I would have died," Tally declared. "Right then and there. Helvetica Grenier sounds terrifying."

"Oh, she can be," Whit said. "Rumor is if you do something to make her really angry, she picks up the phone and makes one call."

There was a pause.

"And . . . ?" I finally asked.

Whit leaned toward me and lowered his voice. "And you'll never work in publishing again. Or fashion. Or movies or TV. Or music. If she decides you're out, then you are all the way out."

I looked at Ivy, who nodded. "I've heard that, too," she said. "But I don't personally know of anybody it's happened to. The reality is, Helvetica Grenier runs one of the most successful magazines in the country, and she takes her job very seriously. So you stay on your best behavior around her, and you hope you don't mess anything up or do anything stupid."

Somehow, all three of us ended up looking at Tally at the same time.

"What?" Tally asked.

"Just don't ever get in the elevator if Helvetica's in it, Tal," I said.

"Which elevator?" Tally asked.

"*Any* elevator," Ivy and Miko said simultaneously.

"I don't know what the four of you are getting so stressed about," Dakota said. "Helvetica Grenier deals with top-level stuff. You're four kids from upstate nobody's ever heard of who print some little girls' newsletter for their friends. It's not like you're going to be running into Helvetica. She's got more important things to do than deal with you four girls. And you wouldn't be here at all if Ivy's mother didn't work here."

"And you would still be here if your dad didn't pull strings to get you an internship?" Ivy retorted. "You know nobody's going to turn down the head of business operations when he wants a favor—"

"Knock, knock," came a voice from the doorway.

Whit suddenly slid his feet off the desk and stood up, looking at the door.

A slim, dark-haired man was standing in the doorway, dressed in all black from head to toe. He was so small I might have mistaken him for a child, except for the little mustache and goatee he was sporting.

"Am I interrupting something?" he asked, his tone indicating that the answer had better be no.

"We were just going over some of the rules for our guests, Garamond," Dakota said. "And making sure they know to stay out of Helvetica's way."

"Well, that's not going to be possible," Garamond said. "Because I'm supposed to bring them up to Helvetica's office right now. Oh, Ivy Scanlon, there you are," he said. "Don't you look adorable. How's the country treating you, darling?"

Ivy stood up. "It's great. It's so good to see you again, Garamond. It's been a while."

"You were just a fifth-grader the last time I saw you.

But you still have that perfect peaches-and-cream complexion, just like your mother. Who I just spoke to, by the way. She wanted to make sure I escorted you to Helvetica's office myself."

"What does she want to see them for?" asked Dakota, putting her hands on her hips.

I was curious, too, since Helvetica had already introduced herself to us, but I wasn't going to wait around asking about it. I followed Ivy to the door, with Miko and Tally right behind me.

As we left the office, Ivy shot a look over her shoulder at Dakota.

"Guess maybe we four girls are a little bit important after all!" she said to me, but from the look on Dakota's face, I was pretty sure she'd overheard.

· chapter ·

4

Garamond kept looking back at us as we followed him, like he was afraid he'd lose one of us. His shoes squeaked with each step he took down the hall. There was no losing him.

I took Ivy's arm and pulled her toward me. "So who's Whit?" I whispered.

She shot me a look, and to my surprise I saw her face had gone pink. I had never seen Ivy blush before.

"Later," she mouthed, and I nodded. So there WAS a story to go with the adorable Whit! I couldn't wait to hear it.

"What a day, and it isn't even over yet," Garamond said. "I had to come in two hours early to conference call with Paris. Not that they ended up being on time."

"Oh, do you speak French?" Miko asked.

Garamond stopped at an elevator and pushed UP,

then gave Miko an appraising look.

"*Mais bien sûr,*" he said. "*Et vous?*"

"*Oui, je parle un peu,*" Miko said. "I've wanted to go to Paris since I was three years old."

"Oh, you must go," Garamond said. "There is no place quite like Paris the first time you see it. Are you interested in fashion?"

The elevator arrived with a quiet *ping*, and the doors slid smoothly open.

Miko looked pleased and embarrassed at the same time. "I am, actually," she said.

"I knew it," Garamond said with satisfaction as we stepped into the elevator. "You've got a good eye. I can tell just by looking at a person. We need to make sure you get to see the sample room while you're visiting. You'll lose your mind over some of the things in there!"

"Oh, do you think I'd be able to take a picture of it for our magazine?" Miko asked.

"I'm not in charge of the sample room, but I could put in a good word for you," Garamond told her as the elevator came to a stop. "Let me see what I can work out."

This was great for Miko; I could tell she wanted to jump up and down with excitement. And if we got a shot of the famous sample room for the magazine, it would be great for *4 Girls,* too!

There was another *ping*, and the elevator opened to reveal a gleaming white lobby. The walls were lined with magazine covers, framed and dating back to the very first issue of *City Nation*. There was a sitting area of snow-white upholstered chairs near gleaming glass doors. *Who would ever sit there?* I wondered. I'd be afraid I'd leave a bit of ink or dirt or something if I even touched one.

Garamond took us through the doors, where twin desks flanked a short corridor, at the end of which was a closed door. One of the desks was empty. At the other sat a young woman with huge, green eyes and shiny, honey-colored hair pulled up in a French twist. The phone was ringing as we walked toward the desk. The woman pointed at Garamond, then pointed at a row of silver and leather chairs along one wall. A small plaque on her desk read CONSTANTIA DAVID, ASSISTANT TO MS. GRENIER.

Constantia, Garamond, Helvetica. Where did *City Nation* people get these names?

"Have a seat," Garamond whispered while we waited for Constantia to be ready for us.

"Helvetica Grenier's office," she said in a voice that was both calming and authoritative at the same time. "No, you'll have to push that back. No, that's simply not possible. She's in with the camera crew right now."

"Camera crew?" asked Tally a little louder than she probably meant to.

Garamond actually jumped at the sound. Her voice echoed in the silent office. I hissed Tally's name, and Ivy actually stuck her hand over Tally's mouth.

Our friend stared at us, her cornflower-blue eyes huge. Ivy finally took her hand away and whispered, *"Shhhhh."*

Tally looked like she'd accidentally launched a missile. "Sorry," she whispered, still louder than the rest of us. "I didn't mean to."

"You'll be fine," Miko told her. "Just calm down. You're about to see Helvetica Grenier's office! Quiet excitement is key." She gave Tally an encouraging smile, but I could tell Tally was still nervous.

The doors to the lobby opened, and Mrs. Scanlon came in.

"Oh, good," she said. "You're all here. Something came up, and Helvetica thought it might work to include you four in it. She wants to tell you herself, though. Tally, my goodness, you look like you've just seen a ghost. Are you okay?"

"I'm fine," Tally whispered so low that Ivy's mother actually had to lean in closer to hear her.

"Karen, they're adorable," Garamond said, gesturing toward us. "Did you know this one is a fashionista? And Miko is a great name for a designer.

49

And Ivy looks gorgeous! Who's styling her?"

Mrs. Scanlon laughed. "She styles herself, and you know it, Gare," she said.

"No!" Garamond said, sounding scandalized. He lifted his eyebrows dramatically, then winked at Ivy.

The intercom on Constantia's desk buzzed. She pushed a button, murmured something, and then gestured to Garamond, who leaped to his feet.

"She wants you now," Garamond told us, smoothing back his jet-black hair. In the bright overhead lights, I could see it had been dyed, and a tiny bead of sweat had appeared at the very top of his forehead.

"Go right in, please," said Constantia.

Tally pressed her lips together tightly, apparently in an attempt to stifle any loud noises she might accidentally make. I tugged one of her curls lightly, and when she turned around, I stuck my tongue out at her. That seemed to relax her a little.

Garamond walked in ahead of us, his shoes squeaking to announce his arrival.

Helvetica's office was a huge room in the corner of the building, and two walls were nothing but glass. Sunlight streamed in, and New York City was displayed in all its glory outside—skyscrapers on one side and a huge expanse of a green park on the other. Her desk was a massive ocean liner of wood and shiny metal in front of the center of one window. Lit from behind, Helvetica looked like a purple-clad celestial superbeing.

We were not the only people in her office. There was a man standing in the corner of the room. Most of his head was obscured by a large video camera with a red light blinking at us. As I tried to figure out what was going on, he pointed the camera at us. I could see a tiny woman who had been standing behind him staring at us with her hands on her hips.

"Just pretend like you're not on camera," the man said.

"They're not on camera yet," Helvetica said. "And they won't be unless I have specifically said so." The man instantly turned the camera off and took a step backward.

"What I wanted to explain to you girls is that we are being filmed for an episode of a documentary television show called *One Week*. This episode will follow the staff at *City Nation* for one week as we go about our business. Naturally, we have the right of approval over any sequences used. Since you girls are here this week representing your magazine, I'd like the camera crew to film you occasionally *if* you happen to cross paths. We'd like to show that there are opportunities here for young people as well as experienced professionals, and since your visit coincides with filming, I think it would be nice to include you. What do we think?"

"We'd be honored," I blurted out. Then I looked at my friends, hoping they felt the same way.

"Yes, thank you," Miko agreed as Ivy and Tally both nodded.

"Excellent," Helvetica said. "Now you can start, Bob. Vicky, you'll have the paperwork."

The cameraman had the camera focused on us by the time I turned back to look at him. *This is unexpected*, I thought. If only we could show ourselves being filmed for our readers.

Well, why not? I thought. Though my heart had already started pounding with nervousness, I decided to speak up.

"Ms. Grenier, is there any way we could take a little video right now, too? It would be incredible for our *4 Girls* readers to be able to share this moment with us. Here we are standing in your office, and there's a film crew here . . ."

Helvetica gave me an approving smile. "I like the way you think, Paulina. That's a great idea. And, yes, of course you can. You can start recording right now, if you'd like."

I shot a look in Miko's direction. She was already pulling her little video camera out of her bag. First she pointed it at Tally, but Tally was staring at Bob and didn't seem to notice the rest of us. So Miko pointed it at me and mouthed, "Say something."

This was not exactly what I had in mind. I didn't really want to be on camera performing by myself! But the moment was too good to miss, so I took a deep breath and began talking.

"Hi, 4 Girls readers and bloggers. You will never guess where we are right now. We're standing in the office of the legendary editor in chief of City Nation magazine, Helvetica Grenier. We've just learned that the magazine is being filmed by a crew from a documentary show this week, and it's possible that 4 Girls might show up on it! So even though we've only been here for about an hour, things are already getting exciting. Stay tuned, and we'll keep posting video updates with the latest!"

Miko quickly panned the camera around the office to take everything in. Then she turned the camera off. "Are we allowed to show you and your office on our web issue?" Miko asked Helvetica. "If it's not okay, I'll just edit that last part out."

"You're absolutely right to ask, Miko," Helvetica said. "You have very good reporter instincts. Yes, you may show all the footage you take in our offices, including any I show up in. And to give you an idea of how we clear that professionally, I'll have Constantia give you a release form that will serve as written permission for you to film here. It's the same form we signed for the *One Week* crew. In return, you four will need to sign a release, too, saying that you agree to be included on the program. Karen has already spoken to your parents to make sure it's okay with them, so now it's fully your choice."

There was a brief pause. Helvetica folded her hands on her desk and stared at us expectantly. She was very clearly done.

"Wonderful," Mrs. Scanlon said. "This is really terrific for the girls, Helvetica."

"Oh, yes, thank you so much for everything, and for taking the time to meet with us today," I said quickly. My mother must have reminded me a hundred times before I left to say thank you to everybody. I still felt a little nervous speaking to Helvetica, but I figured if I was going to get through the next couple days, I'd better get used to it.

"Yes, thank you!" Miko said.

"We know how busy you are," Ivy added.

The three of us looked at Tally. She looked frozen to the floor but slowly nodded her head. I started to feel a little bad. It was weird for Tally to not be her bubbly, friendly self. We'd only wanted her to be . . . quieter. I decided I would pull her aside later to help her relax a little more.

"I'll make sure to get that location information you

wanted e-mailed to you right away," Mrs. Scanlon said to Helvetica, placing one hand on my back and one hand on Miko's and applying the tiniest bit of pressure. Time for us to leave. Garamond was already halfway out the door, his shoes still squeaking every time he took a step. We followed him out, single file.

"Have fun, girls," Helvetica called. "And, Garamond, for heaven's sake, do something about those shoes!"

· chapter ·

5

"So now we're going to split up," Mrs. Scanlon explained to us once we were back in the lobby.

We gathered around her like little sheep, ready to follow her lead. Through the glass doors, I could still see Constantia taking multiple phone calls while typing and pulling out files at the same time. Everyone was so busy! It almost made school, *4 Girls*, watching Kevin, and helping Mom at home seem like a breeze.

"Paulina and Tally, you're going to come with me to a content meeting that is going on right now. Miko and Ivy, Garamond is going to take you to design where they're going over some photos from Fashion Week and deciding which new designer might make for a good feature. We'll meet again in about an hour. Sound good?"

"Yep," Ivy said. Miko was absolutely speechless

with delight over her assignment. She nodded, a wide smile lighting up her face.

"Great. You'll be on this floor. Paulina and Tally, we need to go down two floors. All set, Garamond?"

"Of course," he said, leading Miko and Ivy toward a hallway in the opposite direction from Helvetica's office. "So you two are going to love this," he was saying. "We have several very talented possibilities. There's this new kid whose first line was shown at the tents this year. He's Turkish, you know, and he uses these delicious colors and silks. The only problem is, he's just about the rudest person in the entire world! But, oh, can he drape! During the show, he actually told someone to—"

The rest of the story was cut off as Tally and I stepped into the elevator with Mrs. Scanlon. I was sure Miko and Ivy would get all the details for the blog, at least whatever details they were allowed to use. I couldn't wait to hear more about it.

"So you're going to sit in a meeting where some of our junior editors and writers can pitch ideas for stories," Mrs. Scanlon told us. "Helvetica doesn't go to these meetings. That sometimes makes people feel more comfortable talking about their ideas. I think it will be really interesting for you to see the process. And listen, if one of you has something to say, I want you to be sure to speak up."

"Okay," I said, feeling a flutter of nerves in my stomach. I couldn't imagine any of my ideas would be good for *City Nation*. I looked at Tally. She was practically green, her lips pressed so tight they may have been glued, and her eyes wide as saucers. "Tally, that means you, too. We never meant for you to be absolutely silent the whole time. Just the volume could be lower. Like being in class and giving an answer."

"Oh, I could *never* say something in a meeting," Tally told me. "I'd be too nervous in front of all those people."

"Why, Tally Janeway!" Mrs. Scanlon said as the elevator doors opened. "I've seen you onstage in front of hundreds of people singing your heart out. I can't imagine you being nervous to speak up in front of a few editors."

"But that's different," Tally explained. "That's acting."

We were back on the floor where the interns' office was. The receptionist was busy sorting a stack of mail and waved us through.

"The thing is, it's all acting," Mrs. Scanlon said. "Act like you're not nervous to share your ideas. You'd probably be great at it."

We walked through a large room of low cubicles. All the desks were occupied. There seemed to be more women than men, and everyone was typing or talking on the phone or reading. Some seemed to be doing all three at the same time.

"Here we go," Mrs. Scanlon told us, stopping by a door. "They know we're coming. Just go in quietly and find a place to sit."

The conference room was bright and sunny. Ten or twelve people were sitting around a glossy, honey-colored wood table. On the center was a plate of pastries, though nobody seemed to be eating.

"I just don't think people are going to be interested in another rock-star-turned-activist story," a slim, raven-haired woman with enormous peacock feather earrings and an emerald-green beret was saying.

There were two empty chairs at the table, and Mrs. Scanlon gestured for us to take them. One or two people looked at me and smiled, but everyone else seemed oblivious to the fact that we'd joined them.

"What about a celebrity playlist?" asked a severe, red-haired woman holding an unopened bottle of water in one hand. "We contact twenty or so big names—actors, musicians, writers—and ask them what they're listening to. We can do links to all the bands, and maybe have an online listening option on the website."

"*Vanity Fair* just did that three months ago," a goofy-looking guy with huge black-rimmed glasses pointed out. "And not everybody can relate to playlists. What about what they're reading?"

"Let's refer back to the memo," said the woman with the peacock earrings. "We've got two areas Helvetica thinks we should be looking at—older readers who want a little substance once in a while and are less tech savvy and younger women who want to know what's absolutely the latest thing and are very tech savvy. We've got surveys that show we're losing readers from both of those groups. The older readers opt for *The New Yorker* and the younger ones end up buying *Vogue*, or more often, they just choose to go to the Internet for online publications."

I pulled a little notebook and pen from my bag so I could take detailed notes on the conversation. I'd never thought about reaching different readership through content. I'd have to ask Ivy how we could do this for *4 Girls*. I also wrote myself a note to double-check with Mrs. Scanlon to make sure nothing I might hear about in the meeting would cause a problem if we included it in an article. Were we allowed to mention the names of other magazines? Not that I expected anyone from *Vogue* or *The New Yorker* to care about the *4 Girls* blog, but if there was one thing I'd learned so far, it was to double-check everything. Better safe than very, very sorry.

"Well, let's not forget this month's cover story,"

said the goofy-looking guy. "She's not going to be bringing us much of a crossover audience."

Tally and I exchanged a look. Were we finally going to find out who the mystery celeb was? At least now we knew it was a *she*!

"True. What else have we got?" asked the dark-haired woman.

Everyone seemed to be frantically searching their iPads, tablets, and phones.

"Ten Christmas gifts for readers on a budget?" someone suggested.

"I've seen two of those just this week," Goofy Glasses Guy said. "And we did it last Christmas."

Suddenly everyone began talking at once. The red-haired woman rapped her hand on the table.

"People, come on. We've been sitting here for an hour, and all I'm hearing are the same basic ideas coming from the same people. How difficult can it be to come up with something fresh? Think multigenerational, think broad spectrum, and think holidays."

"That's too broad a spectrum," said Peacock Feather Earrings. "There's no common element that will pull all of these different kinds of people in. I mean, what do they all have in common?"

"You could do pairs," someone said.

Everyone in the room, including me, turned to look

at the person who spoke. Tally immediately smacked one hand over her mouth. "Sorry," she mumbled.

"What do you mean, Tally?" Mrs. Scanlon asked, giving her an encouraging smile.

Tally looked around nervously, like she was thinking of bolting from the room.

"By the way, in case you haven't all figured it out, these are two of our four student guests," Mrs. Scanlon said. "Tally Janeway and Paulina Barbosa. They publish their own magazine at their school, and it's a very good one."

"Finally! People we haven't heard from before," said Goofy Glasses Guy. "So what pears are you talking about? Fruit doesn't sell advertising."

Tally had gone very still. *She really* is *nervous,* I thought.

"Tal, it's only acting," I whispered, reminding her of what Mrs. Scanlon had said.

Tally gave me a blank look, then suddenly something came over her face. A look I had seen before. Tally had something to say.

"Well, if you wanted different ages, you could approach the celebrities like you said and ask them what they're reading, what they're listening to, and what they're wearing, maybe, but you could also ask them to give you a family member who's much older or younger and get their list, too. I love to see pictures

62

of famous people with their parents or kids and hear about them. It's fun to compare."

"Hmm," said Goofy Glasses Guy.

"Write it down," said the red-haired woman. "It's not exactly what we need, but if we play with it, it could turn into something. Marina, shoot it around to the copywriters and see what they can mock up. We won't know if it will work until we can see all the ways it won't. Something might come of it. Oh, and have them text . . . I'm sorry, what was your name?"

Tally started, realizing the red-haired woman was looking at her. "Tally Janeway," she said. "With two *l*s. In Tally, I mean. Janeway doesn't have any *l*s, although sometimes people think my name is—"

"Have them text Tally Janeway, with two *l*s, for some examples of pairs that would appeal to her as a reader. Karen, do you have her contact info?"

Mrs. Scanlon was typing something into her phone.

"Yep, I just forwarded it to the department," she said.

"Good," the woman told her. "Now we've spent way too much time on this already, and it's almost five o'clock. We need to move on to other things. There may be a problem with the piece on the reversible dog coats. The First Lady showed up in a story on CNN holding her dog that was wearing one. They got hit with thousands of requests by the next morning, and their website couldn't handle the traffic and crashed. I need someone else to come up with a quirky handmade pet accessory that we can feature instead, and I need it yesterday."

Neither Tally nor I had any ideas to offer for this or the other stories that came up, like whether an article on gyms would encourage readers or make them feel guilty. I sat quietly taking notes, still hardly able to believe that Tally had just boldly come up with an idea at a *City Nation* content meeting that was the *only* one everyone didn't hate. Our glimpse at the editorial department had definitely gone better than I expected!

As the meeting came to an end, I wondered if Miko and Ivy had done as well in their design meeting. I bet Miko had some great ideas to share, if they asked her to contribute. A shiver of excitement ran through me. We weren't just shadowing people at *City Nation*. We were actually influencing content. Just us four girls.

· chapter ·

6

"I've got to go to a meeting with the photographer's assistant, but I don't want you girls to starve," Ivy's mother told us. "What do you guys think about this dinner plan: We all go downstairs for Chinese—the Wok Emporium is practically part of *City Nation*, so many of us go there. I'll sit at one table and have my meeting, and you guys can get your own table and order whatever you want off the menu. Miko and Ivy will meet us there. Sound good?"

My stomach growled at exactly that moment. "It sounds amazing," I said. "I'm really hungry."

"Me too," Tally said.

"Garamond texted," Mrs. Scanlon said. "He's already waiting for us with Ivy and Miko in the restaurant."

The Wok Emporium was right next door to *City Nation*. As soon as we walked in, we saw

Ivy and Miko sitting at a big table near the window. Garamond hovered nearby, checking his phone. Almost everything in the restaurant was red and gold. The walls were painted with murals of glimmering dragons, and the ceiling was festooned with bright paper lanterns. I loved it.

"Oh good, you're here," Garamond said, hurrying over to meet us. "Karen, they were fabulous, but I can't stick around to brag about them. If I don't get upstairs right now, there may be an armed rebellion in the marketing department. Phoebe is here and waiting for you, but she dashed into the ladies' room. Can't stop! Running! Dashing!"

"A rebellion? Was he serious?" Tally asked, watching Garamond fly out the door with an expression of appreciation that only one truly dramatic person could have for another.

"Partly," said Mrs. Scanlon. "Garamond is the managing editor. Part of his job is making sure everything stays on schedule and everyone is doing what they're supposed to be doing. Sometimes that involves finding the drama and playing peacemaker."

"You'd be good at that, Tal," I said. "At least the drama part."

"Oh, there's Phoebe. If you need anything, I'll be right over there." Mrs. Scanlon waved and headed over to her table.

"Ivy! Miko! How did it go?" I called out when we were almost to the table.

"It was *amazing*," Miko said excitedly. "They showed us the most beautiful portfolios, plus video of some of the collections from Fashion Week. We saw some gorgeous clothes."

"And some hideous ones," Ivy added, handing over a menu. "Sit down, you two, and decide what you want. I've been craving Wok Emporium dumplings for months."

"That's very cool of your mom to let us have our own table," I said to Ivy.

"She used to practically live here," Ivy replied. "Everyone from the magazine comes here for working meals. What are you going to have?"

"I don't know yet," I said.

"I want moo goo gai pan because I love the name," Tally said.

"Guys, guess who came up with a suggestion at the content meeting that they actually took seriously?" I said.

"Oh, Paulie, that's great!" Ivy exclaimed.

"It wasn't me. It was Tally," I announced proudly.

"This I have to hear," Miko said.

"Paulina, there's the waiter. Do you know what you want?" Ivy asked. "I'm going to go crazy if I don't get those dumplings soon."

I had still not even looked at the menu. "I guess I'll have the moo goo gai pan, too," I said, not wanting to keep everyone waiting. I had no idea what it was. I hoped it didn't turn out to be something gross like squid.

Ivy waved at the waiter and expertly ordered for the table, while Tally explained her idea to Miko.

"So it was really what they had already talked about, but in pairs," Tally was saying. "Like mother/daughter. Or son/grandmother. Don't you love it when you see a picture of a famous person with their family? I love seeing if they look alike and how normal it all seems while totally not being normal."

"Tally, that's amazing that you had the nerve to speak up," Miko said. "Good for you."

"Amazing that Tally had the nerve?" Ivy asked, leaning forward. "You guys should have heard Miko. She was talking like she was a fashion editor herself. I had no idea how much she knows about fashion. At one point Garamond opened this one portfolio, and Miko pointed at the dresses and said, 'It looks like an early Marimekko print,' and everybody was agreeing with her and saying how she was exactly right."

"Well, everyone knows Marimekko," Miko said.

Tally and Ivy looked at each other.

"Nobody at this table does," Ivy stated.

"It's seriously so amazing, though," Miko said, her face flushed with happiness. "The people at this meeting really knew their designers. I was in awe just listening to them. And they do this thing a couple times a year where they pick a young, basically unknown designer and feature them in the magazine. It can completely change a designer's life if they get picked, and I sort of . . . helped."

"That will make an incredible story for *4 Girls*," I said. "We can write about the winner, too!"

"Actually, we can't," Miko said. "I was careful to check on what we can and can't use. We can't write about the winner because it won't be announced in *City Nation* until December, and we can't use photographs of any of the designs. Even *City Nation* has to get permission in writing for every design they show."

I tried not to look disappointed. I'd already been envisioning what a cool montage we could do of designs and the closest contenders to the winner.

"But we did a video log, showing the room, which is where the designers actually come when they bring their collections to show in person, and Miko interviewed Garamond," Ivy added. "There's plenty of good stuff to use."

"Are we going to upload that to the site

tonight?" Tally asked, pulling the wrapper off her chopsticks and folding it into a tiny paper airplane.

"Oh, we definitely should," I said. "I think that's part of the really cool aspect of this web issue—it's kind of unfolding as it happens."

"Miko, I have to try on that jacket and the dress you said I could borrow," Tally said. "I can't keep showing up on video in this."

"Well, you can't do that until we get back to the hotel," I said. "Anyway, you don't have to worry. No more cameras for now."

"Don't be too sure," Ivy said, pointing at the door. I turned to see what Ivy was pointing at.

Bob the Camera Guy and Vicky the Producer were coming through the door. Vicky made a beeline for the counter, but Bob noticed us and came over.

"Hey, it's the four magazine girls," he said.

"Are we being taped?" Tally asked.

Bob laughed and patted a large bag slung over his shoulder. "Nope. Both my cameras are packed up in here," he said. "We just came by for takeout. Everybody recommended this place. Although actually, it would make a nice shot—the four of you sitting in here waiting for dinner and talking about your day at the magazine. Can you guys look like that's what you're doing?"

"That IS what we're doing," I told him. He was

nice enough, I guess, but Bob was kind of an odd duck. I wondered how the footage for *One Week* would come out.

"Even better," Bob said. "I'm going to go place my order, then I'll be right back to set up the shot."

Tally was trying to check her reflection in the window, making sure she was camera-ready. "Oh look, Whit and Dakota are walking by!" Tally exclaimed. She leaned over to the window and started banging on the glass and waving.

"Oh, Tally, don't. Stop it," Ivy said, looking dismayed.

"They're coming in," Tally said, turning to us with a smile. Then she saw our faces. "I'm sorry. Should I not have done that?"

Ivy glanced at me, then looked away and shrugged. "Whatever. They're here now."

They were, and they were already headed for our table. Whit was dressed in the same beige Dockers and blue sweater he'd been wearing earlier, but Dakota had changed into a stretchy knit dress of rose- and cream-colored swirls and high suede boots. I envied both her outfit and the self-assured manner in which she carried it off.

"Thanks for keeping us in suspense," Whit said, plopping down in the empty chair next to Ivy. "What did Helvetica want?"

"Oh, I'm sorry, Whit. I should have texted to let you know," Ivy said.

"We went straight from her office to our meetings," I explained. "Tally and I went to a content meeting, and Ivy and Miko went to a design meeting. Anyway, she just asked if we'd be okay with appearing on this documentary they're doing, for that show—"

Dakota's mouth dropped open. "Wait. They asked *you* to be on *One Week*?" she asked.

"They said it would be nice to have some young people on it because they have readers our age and they thought they could relate," Tally explained. "I—"

"I *know* that," Dakota interrupted. "They were supposed to be putting me and Whit on the show. We're the actual interns." She glared at Ivy.

"Well, maybe they still will," Ivy said.

Dakota shook her head, looking angry. "No. All the releases had to be requested and signed by today. *I* know that because *I* had to type up the in-house memo about it. Garamond said they'd almost definitely be asking us, then you guys show up and we're history. I can't believe this!"

"Look, that isn't fair, I'll agree," Miko said. "I'd be disappointed, too, but it's not like we asked. We didn't even know about it."

"It's only a stupid TV show, Dakota," Whit said.

"I'm only saying—" Dakota's voice dropped off suddenly. Bob had paid for his dinner and was walking toward us, camera in hand and the red light illuminated.

We were all sitting there staring at him.

"Don't look at me," Bob said. "Don't look at the camera. Just act natural. Wait a minute, where did those other two come from? I wanted just the *City Nation* shot."

Dakota gave a gasp of irritation. "Just the *City Nation* shot? I can't believe you guys. I don't know why they invited you in the first place, unless your mother begged them to, Ivy. I've seen your stupid magazine. For the life of me I can't figure out what the big deal is. I'm out of here."

Dakota stood up and turned to grab her purse, and for just a moment I thought I saw tears in her eyes. It did seem kind of unfair that we had apparently replaced the real interns as the representative young faces of the magazine.

"Whit, come on," Dakota said. He showed no signs of getting up.

Bob was impatiently shifting from one foot to the other.

"Oh, I uh . . . I thought I might . . ." Whit glanced uncertainly at Ivy.

Hey, I thought. *What is up with that?*

"You said you'd let me borrow your MetroCard. I left mine at home," Dakota pressed.

"It's okay. We'll see you tomorrow," Ivy told Whit.

"People? I don't mean to be rude, but are we doing this or not?" Bob asked.

As soon as Whit stood up, Dakota stalked off to the door.

"Sorry about that," Whit said. "She can be kind of touchy. Catch you guys tomorrow."

As soon as Whit walked away from the table, Bob snapped the camera up and pointed it right at us. "Okay," Bob said. "Look like you're having fun."

Even Tally didn't seem to know how to spontaneously do that. Fortunately the waiter chose that moment to arrive with our dinner.

"Oh, those dumplings smell amazing!" I exclaimed. Ivy had ordered enough for all of us. And as I removed the little dome from the plate put in front of me, I saw a delicious steaming concoction of chicken and mushrooms and vegetables.

"Everybody has to use chopsticks. It's good luck!" Tally announced.

I tried to pick up a piece of chicken with mine, but every time I got it just about to my lips, it dropped back onto the plate.

"Give her a fork," Ivy said, laughing.

"No, no forks!" Tally insisted.

"Paulina, look. Watch me," Miko said. "Hold the chopsticks like this."

I mimicked what Miko was doing, picked up a piece of chicken, and could almost taste it when it slipped out of the chopsticks again. I groaned as Miko chuckled, and Tally protested as Ivy handed me a fork.

"Perfect!" Bob said. "That's exactly what I needed. You guys look like you're just unwinding after a long day of work and having some fun."

It was no act. That was *exactly* what we were doing.

· chapter ·

7

"Okay, now that I finally have you alone, what is the deal with Whit? How come you've never mentioned him?" I asked as I jumped onto my bed and faced Ivy.

Ivy smacked her hands over her face. "I had no idea Whit was going to be there," she said. "I knew we'd be seeing Dakota, but I didn't know Whit was interning this year."

"So?" I pressed. "How well do you know him?"

"Well, like Whit said, all three of us had been in school together since kindergarten. My mom and Whit's mom and Dakota's dad all started working at *City Nation* around the same time, and we were all enrolled at the Montessori school a few blocks away. So we were sort of friends the way you are when you're little, right? Like people you might not necessarily get along with when you're older. Like I said, Dakota's supercompetitive, and she always has been. But we coexisted *okay*. Then, for some reason, she kind of turned on me last year. She stirred up a bunch of trouble and got a group of girls to stop talking to me, then she tried to get Whit on her side and to get his friends to stop talking to me, too. For, like, no reason. But by then, my parents already had this plan to move, and after a month or so most people were forgetting they weren't supposed to talk to me, so I just kind of let it go. But it really upset me. To this day, I have no idea what set her off."

"Any chance it might have been Whit?" I asked.

"What? Why would you say that?" Ivy asked, though her cheeks were starting to turn pink again.

"Well, I was kind of getting the impression that *she* likes Whit," I said. "And Whit obviously likes you. So . . ."

Ivy's cheeks flushed bright red then. "He *obviously* likes me? Where did that come from?"

"Well, just from the way he acts around you," I said. "Like how he looks at you when someone else is talking. He pays attention to you. He just kind of gets sparkly when you're around."

"Sparkly?" Ivy repeated, laughing.

I laughed, too. "No, I know, but you know what I mean, right?"

"About sparkly? In a bizarre way, yes. But you think Whit might really like me?"

"I'm just telling you the vibe I was getting," I said. "Would that be a good thing? If he liked you?"

Ivy looked thoughtful. "It sure would have been if I hadn't moved," she said. "But he lives three hours away from me now. I mean yeah, obviously it would be a good thing, but . . . it would be kind of a bummer, too."

"New York's not that far away," I pointed out. "And your mom is working here again now. Who knows—you could end up spending the summer here. It could happen, right?"

"It could, I guess," Ivy agreed. "I don't know."

"Well, I *do* know," I said. "You were pushy with me when I didn't want to do anything about Benny Novak, and you were right! He ended up asking me out. So now I'm being pushy with you about Whit."

Ivy smiled at me.

"Thanks," she said. "I really was surprised to see him. Everything was happening so fast."

"Yeah, what a long and crazy day," I said.

"And it's not over yet," Ivy reminded me. "We've still got work to do. What is taking Miko and Tally so long, anyway?"

Ivy started fiddling with her cell phone.

"What are you doing?" I asked her.

"I'm texting them."

I laughed at Ivy's laziness. "Don't strain yourself or anything," I said.

I could actually hear Tally's squeals in the next room, and moments later the door to our room burst open and they came in.

"Sorry we took so long," Tally apologized. "Miko was helping me try on those things of hers. She brought so many clothes, I'll have something new to wear every day! I'm glad I forgot my suitcase!"

Miko rolled her eyes. "And I watched the video I shot today. I should be able to upload it with just a few easy edits I can do on my laptop," she said.

"Awesome," Ivy told her. "Okay, so are you guys ready?"

"Explain it again," Tally said.

"We're going to answer questions people have posted on the blog, but instead of typing them like we usually do, we're going to record our responses on video."

"I'll set up the webcam shot. Paulina, why don't you pull the blog up on your laptop?" Ivy said. "I hope people actually posted questions. I didn't want to look beforehand because I want the whole thing to feel spontaneous, you know? Like the readers are really interviewing us. Okay, everybody squish together on the bed."

"Don't forget to leave room for Ivy," I pointed out as Tally sprawled beside me.

"That's good. This will get all four of us. I'm turning the camera on."

Seconds later, we were all squeezed in next to each other on the screen, smiling at the webcam.

"*4 Girls* here," Ivy said. "We're coming to you from our hotel on West Forty-Second Street, and boy, have we had a long day."

"Later tonight we'll post an article and a video about our experiences in the editorial and design departments at *City Nation* today," I added. "Be sure to check back for those. In the meantime, we've got a little free time, and we've been dying to check the blog to see who's got questions for us."

I had my laptop open, half on my lap and half on Tally's. I had already opened the blog and clicked through to the thread we'd started for questions and answers. I was relieved to see four questions had already been posted. I nudged Tally, and she cleared her throat.

"Okay, question one is from Puppyfan29. 'I saw a movie about someone working at a magazine in New York, and they showed all the people as either mean or snooty. What are the people at *City Nation* like?' That's a great question. Thanks, Puppyfan. I feel like we met all kinds of different people today. The people in the editorial department were all different ages, but I would say I saw more people that were dressed kind of quirky or stood out in some way. Definitely everybody is really smart."

"The design associates I met were all super well-dressed, no big surprise," Miko said. "I guess they could sort of appear intimidating at first, but they were all really cool and nice to me. I think they're all just really psyched to work at *City Nation*."

Satisfied with our answers, I read the next question.

"'From what you've seen so far, do you think *City Nation* is a cool place to work? Would you want to work there?' Good question from PinkyPie. I'd have to say yes to both. *City Nation* is known for its writing, current events pieces, photography, fashion coverage, and editorials. If you're a creative person and you want to work for a really high-level group, I think you'd be crazy to *not* want to work there. As some of you know, Ivy's mom does work there, so maybe Ivy wants to add something more."

Ivy nodded. "Yes to everything Paulina said, but also it can be tough. They expect you to be the best because *they* are the best. So if you want to work at *City Nation*, you have to stay on your toes."

"Now one more question, from CaptainPony," Miko said, leaning forward to read the screen. "'Have you found out who is going to be on the cover yet? Are you still each getting to ask that person a question?' We still have no idea, but the photo shoot is scheduled for tomorrow, so keep checking back. When we know, you'll know!"

"So that's about all we have to report for tonight," Ivy said. "Tomorrow we're due back at *City Nation* at nine AM, and we're prepared for anything. Whatever happens, we'll be sure to keep all of you in the loop. Until then, New York hellos from your favorite *4 Girls*."

Tally blew a kiss, and Miko and I waved, then Ivy got up and switched the webcam off.

"Cool," she said. "I think that went well."

"It did," I said. "Though I feel like I sound funny when I talk on camera."

"Oh no, you sounded like a pro!" Tally reassured me.

"Mmm, if you say so," I answered. "Wow, I'm really exhausted."

"We should all get some sleep," Ivy said. "I was serious when I said we have to be prepared for anything tomorrow. It's going to be a long day, and we all have to be at our absolute best."

Ivy went to say good night to her mother. I yawned, changed into my pajamas, and crawled into bed. I was only too glad to get some rest, but my mind was racing from all the crazy excitement of *City Nation*.

The faces of Garamond and Constantia and Bob and Vicky and Helvetica herself floated through my mind.

Be prepared for anything, I told myself. I was running one hundred different versions of what "anything" might be when I finally fell into a deep, dreamless sleep.

· chapter ·

8

"Now, the thing with a photo shoot day is it's all about the schedule, but we almost always end up off schedule," Mrs. Scanlon explained to us as we walked out of the hotel still munching on our breakfast pastries. "And one of the things that happens more often than you think is the person we are supposed to be shooting is late or misses a flight and can't make it at all. But Garamond has just texted me that she's arrived in the office safe and sound."

"So now can you tell us who it is, Mom?" Ivy said.

Mrs. Scanlon smiled as we stopped at the corner to wait for the light. "It's Quincy Vanderstan."

Tally gasped and smacked both hands over her mouth.

"Quincy Vanderstan?" Miko said. "Wow!"

I had to agree. WOW indeed.

Quincy Vanderstan was the It Girl of the Year. She had rocketed to fame recently as the plucky and beautiful sidekick in *The Time Lord*, a popular sci-fi show. She had been in two feature films since then, both shot this year, and now it seemed her face was everywhere.

"And we're really each going to get to ask her a question for *4 Girls*?" I asked, dodging out of the way of a man with a briefcase shouting into a cell phone. It was morning in Manhattan, and everyone was rushing to work.

"That is still the plan," Mrs. Scanlon said. "What we'll be doing first is going to a pre-shoot meeting. While Quincy is being fitted in wardrobe and having her hair and makeup done, we go through the checklist for every department, right down to making sure lunch is taken care of. There's nothing like waiting until the last minute, only to discover that the person doesn't eat meat or can't stand fish. We have to make sure everything is set. You'd be surprised how many times we get ready to go and find something really basic has been forgotten. Once we had a big shoot scheduled in Central Park. Fourteen models, three photographers, over a hundred dresses. But no one got a permit from the city to do the shoot—they shut us down. That's basic stuff, but somehow it slipped through the cracks. You'll see all the departments reporting in, except for the people working to get Quincy ready."

I tried to take in everything she was saying, but my mind kept going back to Quincy Vanderstan. What question should I ask her? What did I even have to say to somebody that famous?

There were lots of people going into the lobby with us—everybody carrying coffee or a bagel and looking fresh-faced and ready for another day. We had to stop at security again and get new photo identification badges, but soon we were packed into an elevator on our way up to the office. It smelled like perfume and coffee and blueberry muffins.

Mrs. Scanlon took us to the same floor we had first come to yesterday. The receptionist was already there signing for a package while answering the phone and looking as if she had never left her desk all night, except for the fact that she had on a different outfit. When she saw Mrs. Scanlon, she waved us through, still talking on the phone.

"So we'll be in the main conference room with the lighting designer and . . . oh, hang on."

Her phone was ringing, and she answered it quickly.

"I am going to scream when I see Quincy Vanderstan," Tally told us.

"Tally!" Miko and Ivy said simultaneously.

"Oh, I don't mean out loud," Tally corrected. "I'm going to scream inside my brain."

"Guys, seriously, now that we know who she is, we need to come up with our questions. I think we should all share them in advance to make sure two of us aren't going to ask the same thing," I suggested. "I know we all came up with possibilities, but that was when we had absolutely no idea who the person was. I honestly don't like any of the ones I thought of."

"You're right," Ivy said. "Let's . . ." Her voice trailed off. Her mom had just gotten off the phone and was standing with one hand pressed to her head.

"Mom? Is everything okay?" Ivy asked.

Mrs. Scanlon dropped her hand away from her face. "Oh, there's just a bit of a problem, apparently. I was just telling you these things happen, but it's awfully early in the morning for things to go wrong. Anyway, I've got to go help sort this out. Under the circumstances, I think it might be better if you didn't come along for the pre-shoot meeting just yet. Hopefully this will all get set right shortly. Can I ask you all to just sit tight for a bit?"

"Sure. We can go to the intern room and wait there," Ivy said.

"I'll text you or come and get you as soon as we're back on track," Mrs. Scanlon said, doubling back toward the elevator. "Sorry! But such is life at *City Nation*!"

"That didn't sound good. What do you think is going on?" I asked Ivy as we followed her toward the interns' office.

"Oh, you wouldn't believe the things that happen," Ivy told us. "Mom said one time they had special lights flown in from Paris and no electrical adapters to make them work. Nobody had thought of that. Another time there was a mouse in the studio, and the photographer just up and quit right on the spot. But usually it's something easier to deal with. I'm sure it will be fine."

The interns' office was empty when we got there. We each sat down at a desk. Tally put her feet up on the desk and looked around.

"Do you think Helvetica Grenier ever had to work in a little office like this?" she asked.

"She actually did," Ivy said. "She started as an intern in the mail room. Then she got a job as a secretary."

"Wow. That's impressive," Miko said. "I wonder if—"

The door to our little office burst open, and Garamond rushed in. He looked kind of agitated, dressed all in black as he had been the day before. I wondered how many all-black outfits he owned.

"Has anyone been here?" he asked.

We looked at each other. "Since this morning?" Ivy asked.

"Since ever!" Garamond said. He was actually wringing his hands together.

"The office was empty when we got here," Miko said. "But we only just came in."

Garamond turned to go without a word, then stopped. "Call me if you see anything!" he said, then he rushed out the door.

Ivy and I stared at each other.

"Call him if we see WHAT?" I asked. "Do you think this has something to do with the photo shoot?"

"It can't be a coincidence," Ivy said. "Garamond is the one who supervises everyone on a shoot like this, and my mom did just say there was a problem."

"You could just text your mom and ask," Tally suggested.

"No, I don't want to bother her if she's in the middle of something. And this seems big. We'll just hang out and wait like she said to."

"Hey! I thought you guys were with the photo team this morning. How was your dinner?" came a guy's voice.

We turned and saw Whit coming in the door holding a half-eaten bagel. He was talking to all of us, but he was only looking at Ivy.

"Oh, it was better than I remembered," Ivy said. "You should have stayed."

"You're right," Whit said, shutting the door with his foot as he took a bite of his bagel. "There's always the lunch special."

"Oh, are we going back to the Wok Emporium?" Tally asked, her face brightening.

"We don't all have to eat lunch together," I said quickly.

I couldn't help it—now that I knew Ivy liked Whit, and I was so certain he liked her, I wanted them to get together for a lunch date. Maybe if she spent a little time alone with him, she would be able to figure out how she felt about it. I had been able to keep in touch with my friend Evelyn on Skype after she moved away—it was amazing how chatting by webcam could really make you feel like you were with somebody. Maybe Ivy and Whit could do the same. That would certainly guarantee that Dakota wouldn't butt in.

"Well, what's the schedule for you guys today?" Whit asked. "Maybe—"

The office door opened quickly, almost smacking Whit, who stepped quickly out of the way. It was Constantia, Helvetica's assistant.

"Good. You're here," Constantia said. "Has anyone else been in this office today?"

"Garamond was just here," Ivy said.

"Yes, that's fine," Constantia replied. "But . . . no one else?"

"Just us," Tally said. "Is it another mouse?"

Constantia seemed to notice Tally for the first time and gave her a perplexed look. "I'm sorry?" she said. "A mouse?"

"In the studio?" Tally suggested. "Or a bat, maybe? That's worse because they fly. I had one fly right at me once in school. I still haven't recovered. I can't even—"

"I see," Constantia said. "There are no bats at *City Nation*. Where is Dakota?"

"She stopped at reception to talk to some junior editors," Whit said. "I saw her on my way in. Do you need me to get her?"

"No," Constantia said. "But if you see anything unusual, please phone my extension immediately." She shut the door quietly behind her.

"What in the world is going on?" I asked.

Whit shook his head. "I have no idea, but I bet you anything by the time Dakota gets here she'll know all about it. She always gets the gossip first, and she was having a very intense talk when I saw her on my way in. She always knows who to talk to when something is up."

"That's so funny that you said that about the

mouse, Tally," Whit continued. "Rumor has it that actually happened a few years ago, and they had to shut the entire shoot down because the model got hysterical."

"Oh, it's totally true, Whit. My mom was there!" Ivy said. "It wasn't the model that got hysterical. It was the photographer!"

"That's hilarious," he said. "Notice how Constantia said to Tally, 'There are no bats at *City Nation,*' but she didn't say there were no mice?"

"Yes!" Ivy said. "Apparently that was the only time anyone can remember seeing Constantia lose her cool. The photographer took off, and they had to get a junior editor to take the pictures. He was actually a really great amateur photographer, and after that shoot he ended up going professional. All because of a mouse."

"I don't suppose we could use that story in *4 Girls,* Ivy?" Miko asked.

"I have a feeling probably not," Ivy said. "Helvetica wouldn't like it."

The door flew open again, and Dakota came in, her eyes gleaming. She stopped short when she saw us, or rather when she saw Ivy and Whit standing together.

"What's up?" Whit asked. "There's something going on, and I know you know. You *always* do. Something's up with the shoot, right?"

Dakota shrugged, then smiled, looking very pleased with herself.

"Come on. Tell us what you found out," Whit pressed.

"Is it a mouse?" Tally asked. "There aren't any bats here, so if you heard that, it isn't true."

"Seriously, Dakota, what's the deal?" Miko asked. "Whit said you always hear what's going on before anyone else because you know all the people to talk to. Do you or don't you?"

Dakota's smile got bigger. "Oh, I do," she said. She perched herself on the edge of a radiator cover beneath the window.

"Dakota, stop fooling around," Ivy said. "What's going on?"

Dakota glanced at Ivy, ignored her, and turned to Whit instead.

"Okay. So the big photo shoot scheduled for this morning has been very hush-hush, right? There's a supercelebrity that nobody was supposed to know about, but *I* know who it is."

"Quincy Vanderstan," Ivy said.

Dakota frowned. "Well, everyone knows *today*," she said. "I've known for, like, weeks. Anyway, they were worried she wouldn't show up because she had to fly in late last night. They wanted her here at eight this morning just to be sure there was enough time to get her ready even if she was late. They had a B-list celeb lined up just in case."

"And she didn't show?" asked Whit.

Dakota leaned forward and touched his arm.

"No, Whit, she *did*!" Dakota said. "She showed up right on time with her mother, who's her manager. But something happened, and she got really mad. Garamond was trying to fix whatever the problem was, but while all that was going on, Quincy . . . *disappeared*."

"Disappeared?" Tally cried. "You mean she was kidnapped?"

"Oh please," Dakota said. "This is reality, not *Law & Order*. I mean she disappeared herself *on purpose*. She took off. That's why everyone is so upset. One of the highest-profile shoots of the year, there's a documentary film crew wandering around, and Quincy Vanderstan is gone."

"She could be anywhere," I said. "This is one of the biggest cities in the world. They should call the police!"

"Oh no. She couldn't have left the building," Whit said. "That would be impossible—the only way out is taking the elevator to the main lobby, and you have to turn your guest pass in to security when you leave. Plus, when there's a celebrity in the building, they make sure security is really well informed. You wouldn't know it, but they probably have extra people at the desk and are being supercareful that everybody gets checked going in *and* out."

"That's right. She's definitely somewhere here in the building," Dakota agreed.

"So that's why Garamond and Constantia were going room to room and questioning people," Ivy said.

I didn't know whether to feel excited or disappointed. It wasn't every day you got to see real movie-star drama unfolding behind the scenes! But I also really wanted to meet Quincy. And if the shoot was off, obviously so was our chance to ask questions.

"That was supposed to be our biggest story," I said to Ivy.

"What was?" Dakota asked.

"We were going to sit in on the photo shoot and each ask Quincy a question for our magazine," Ivy told her.

"No way," Dakota said. "I've seen the memos. That's a totally closed set. They never would have let you in. I begged Garamond to let me be an assistant just so I could watch, and he said no to me."

"Well, they did," Ivy said. "It was all set up—my mother is coordinating the whole piece and doing the interview herself. Why do you look so surprised?"

"Because you're only getting special treatment because of your mother," Dakota snapped. "And she's managed to mess this up pretty well. Helvetica is going to kill her and Garamond when she finds out about this."

"Hey, Dakota, come on. That's not fair," Whit said. "Quincy Vanderstan is the one that messed this up, not anybody else."

"Whatever," Dakota said. "You know how it goes, Whit. When something goes wrong, somebody at *City Nation* gets the blame. That's just the way Helvetica works."

"Your mom might get in trouble for this?" Tally asked. "But she's so nice, and she's been working so hard. It's not fair!"

Ivy looked genuinely distressed, and Dakota did not look sorry about that. She kept finding reasons to touch Whit. This time she nudged him with her foot.

This whole thing is about Whit, I thought. I was sure that was why Dakota turned nasty on Ivy last year, too. If I had noticed Whit seemed to like Ivy, Dakota couldn't possibly have missed it.

"Ivy, I'm sure it will be fine," I said.

"That's a nice thought, Paulina, but that's not how things work around here, and Ivy knows it," Dakota said. "Helvetica comes in at eleven on Tuesdays, and if Quincy isn't at that shoot, somebody is going to be in *major* trouble. Do you have any idea how much money the magazine loses when they have to cancel a big shoot? Plus, there's the fact that there won't be a cover story."

"Maybe we should go and look for her," Tally suggested.

"Tal, we can't do that. If Garamond and Constantia can't find her, how could we? We can't even find our own way around," I pointed out.

"Ivy knows her way around," Tally said.

"Not that well," Ivy replied. "I've visited plenty of times, but that's different."

"Dakota, you seem to know things nobody else does," Miko said. "You might think of places even Garamond and Constantia won't. I'll bet you could find her."

"Probably. If I felt like it," Dakota said, sitting back down on the window ledge. "But I don't really. There's nothing in it for me."

"Because you can't," Ivy said. "Please. You're an intern. You think you could find somebody the entire company is looking for, when nobody else can? You're full of it."

Dakota stood up and put her hands on her hips. "No, I'm not," she said. "I'm telling you, I could find her if I felt like it."

"Prove it," Ivy shot back.

"It would be really cool if you did find her," Whit said. "Can you even imagine what an epic story that would be? The day Dakota Whittier found Quincy Vanderstan. Forget the mouse—people would talk about it forever."

Dakota stared at Whit for a moment. "You know what? You're right. Okay, here's what I think. There's still a little time. Helvetica will be here at eleven. That leaves an hour and a half. I bet I can figure out where Quincy went and find her before then. Convincing her to go back to the shoot—that's another story."

"Okay," I said. "Let's put our heads together then. We'll worry about what to say to her when we find her."

"Oh, it's *we* now?" Dakota asked.

"Let us help you," I said carefully. "A group of people working together is better than one person on her own."

Dakota looked uncertain, but she finally relented.

"Whatever," she murmured.

"Maybe we should start by thinking about what we know about Quincy," Miko suggested.

"Right!" Tally agreed. "It's like Mrs. Scanlon said. We're all acting, all the time. Quincy is just acting like herself now. I've read tons of interviews and stories about her. We just need to take that information and pretend we are Quincy. Where would I go if I was Quincy Vanderstan and I was at *City Nation* and didn't want to be found?"

"Okay," I said. "I think you're onto something, Tally. So what do we know about her?"

I was sitting on one of the desks, Buddha style. Tally perched on top of another, frowning in thought, and Miko was leaning next to her.

"She's really young," Whit said. "I know that. She hasn't graduated from high school yet. She has to work with a tutor on set to keep up with classes. I read that in *Vanity Fair*."

"I saw that article, too," Ivy said. "It said she's got such a crazy schedule she sometimes has to work seven days a week. She said something about never being able to be alone, not even for a second. Maybe she wanted to be by herself for a bit. What about that glassed-in courtyard behind the cafeteria? They've filled it with all these potted trees and flowers—it's a really nice, quiet place."

"It's closed for three days. They're replacing the skylight windows," Whit said.

"Is there a big conference room or some place where they'd have important meetings? Where maybe there are nice chairs or a couch, somewhere she could just hole up and rest?" I asked.

"The executive conference room is like that," Dakota said. "But that's right between reception and Helvetica's office. Constantia would have looked there first thing. She's obsessed with that conference room."

"Quincy is super into fashion," Miko said. "I know that. She goes to the big shows at Fashion Week, and she's always wearing the latest things. I once saw an interview with her where she said she thought designers had the best job in the world."

"Could she be on one of the floors in the building that aren't *City Nation*'s?" I asked.

Dakota shook her head. "No, our elevators only go to *City Nation* floors. If you wanted to go to a different floor you'd have to go to the lobby and go to a separate elevator bank. She would have had to go past security, and I don't think she could have done that."

"Okay, wait," Tally said suddenly. "Let's get back to the fashion thing. She's obsessed with clothes, and she's at *City Nation*. Where would anybody into clothes want to go? I'm Quincy Vanderstan. Where do I want to go?"

Dakota snapped her fingers and pointed at Tally. "You're absolutely right. That would be the very first place she'd want to go."

"Oh, of course," Miko exclaimed.

"You've lost me," Whit said.

"The sample room!" Dakota and Miko said in unison.

"The sample room?" I asked.

"Totally," Miko said. "Remember yesterday when Dakota was talking about the Louboutins coming in? There is this big room here, just like the one they have at *Vogue* and magazines like that, where designers send over samples of pretty much everything. Dresses, coats, shoes, bags, hats, jewelry, formal gowns. If it's in and it's this year, there will be one in the sample room. But it's not just stuff from *this* year. They've got vintage stuff, too. Chanel gowns, Pucci dresses. I've heard it's like a museum in there."

"That's absolutely right," Dakota said.

"Why do they have so much stuff?" Tally asked.

"Because *City Nation*'s fashion editor has a lot of influence," Dakota said. "I mean, it's not like *Vogue* or anything—they are the final word in fashion. But *City Nation* covers designers a lot, too. If some company or designer sends their latest thing over and *City Nation* ends up writing about it or including it in their 'What's Hot' page or giving it any kind of shout-out, their sales will go through the roof. And every designer in New York wants that. So they all send stuff over."

"Okay, but if that's where all the stuff is kept, wouldn't they have taken Quincy there, anyway? To get her stuff to wear for the photo shoot?" I asked.

"No, they wouldn't!" Ivy said, suddenly excited. "There is always an art director in charge of the look of the photo shoot. They figure all that stuff out way in advance, and it can go back and forth for days. They pick things from the sample room that they think would look good for the shoot, and they show them to Helvetica. She makes the final choices. Whatever she's chosen is pulled from the sample room and brought up to the studio ahead of time. That's one of those things Mom was talking about that has to be taken care of before the shoot."

"That's right," Whit confirmed. "They don't want people picking out stuff and telling the editors what they want to wear. The art director makes those choices for them. Though I'm sure they'd have brought her down there to have a look if she'd asked them."

"Well, you can all sit here talking about it, but there's only one way to find out," Dakota said. "We go and see for ourselves."

"We could just call Constantia, or your mom for that matter, and tell them what we think," I said to Ivy.

"Now where would the fun be in that?" Dakota asked. "I thought the whole point was trying to figure this out for ourselves. I'm going to go look."

"Well, wouldn't someone have already thought of this and gone to look there?" I added.

"Maybe," Dakota said. "But they haven't found her. I've been in that sample room. There are plenty of places to hide if you don't want to be seen. I think we should go and look for ourselves."

It had seemed like a good idea before. But we were

guests at *City Nation*, and the only reason for that was Ivy's mom. I didn't want to do anything that might get us in trouble. But Ivy was nodding now, too.

"I agree. Plus, it isn't just a question of finding Quincy. She was obviously upset about something. She's not all that much older than we are. She might listen to us."

"Well, the sample room is only two floors up," Whit said. "Somebody could go and take a quick peek and see what they see. So the only question is, who goes?"

"*Me*," Dakota said. "No one knows the building better than I do."

"That's true," Ivy said.

"So you and Dakota go," Whit said.

Dakota didn't look thrilled with that idea, but she didn't object. I was guessing she'd rather have Ivy with her than leave her with Whit.

"You come, too, Paulie," Ivy said. "You're great at thinking on your feet."

I wasn't so sure about that. But if Ivy wanted me with her, then I would go. She was my best friend, and I wasn't going to let Dakota try to ruin our fun anymore.

"If you're in, I'm in," I told her, sounding much more confident than I felt.

"Okay, if we're all done bonding now, we need to move," Dakota said. "It's quarter to ten now. Isn't the whole point to try and get Quincy back to the studio before Helvetica arrives?"

"How will y'all know when Helvetica is back?" Tally asked.

"Oh, believe me. *Everyone* in the building knows, from Garamond to the people in the mail room," Whit said.

We were about to get a priceless, uncensored view into the workings of *City Nation* magazine for *4 Girls*. Unfortunately, it was already obvious to me that for those same reasons, we wouldn't be able to write a word about it.

Who will believe it, anyway? I thought, getting up and joining Ivy and Dakota at the door. A secret mission to find an escaped movie star and return her to a photo shoot before Helvetica returned?

I wasn't sure I believed it myself.

· chapter ·
10

Ivy and I were both wearing rubber-soled flats, but Dakota had on a pair of towering heels that made a *clackety-clack* sound that echoed through the hall at a deafening level.

"What?" whispered Dakota.

Ivy pointed at her shoes.

Dakota made a face. "You have got to be kidding me," she said. But Ivy just shook her head.

"Fine. I'll try to tiptoe."

Dakota had briefly explained that our best and fastest option was simply to take the main elevator up two floors to where the sample room was. There weren't a lot of people on our floor since everyone was busy with the photo shoot and the missing movie star. The thirty-fourth floor would be much busier. We would have to get through a room full of cubicles where the junior designers and editorial assistants sat. After that, we'd have a clear shot to the sample room.

We reached the elevators without seeing anyone at all, and Dakota pushed the up button.

"What do we do if there's already someone on the elevator?" I said suddenly.

"Who cares?" Dakota asked.

The usual *ping* told us the elevator had arrived, and as the doors opened, I was startled to see Garamond with a phone pressed to one ear. Dakota could have any number of reasons to be there, but Garamond would know that Ivy and I were roaming the halls when we shouldn't be. I nudged Ivy hard.

Ivy dropped her bag, and we both turned our backs toward the elevator and began picking up the contents.

"Hello?!" Garamond was yelling into his phone. "Are you still there? I can't keep a signal in the elevator. Hello?"

"No, she has not been found!" we heard him shout as the doors slid closed again.

"That was close," I said.

"He's in crisis mode," Dakota said, pressing the button again. "He probably wouldn't have noticed if the queen of England had been standing here."

The next elevator that came was empty. We got in, and Ivy pressed the button for the thirty-fourth floor.

My heart was still pounding from our close call with Garamond. I was not good at sneaking around—my fear of getting caught was too severe. And at the moment, we were only in an elevator. What would happen if someone found us trying to get into the sample room? I began to wish we had thought our plan through a little more thoroughly.

The thirty-fourth floor had no reception area at all.

"Why don't they have a desk like the other floors?" I asked as we stepped out of the elevator.

"This floor isn't open to everyone," Dakota said. "You need to swipe an ID card to open the door."

"Well, where would Quincy have gotten one of those?" I asked.

"You need them to open some of the bathrooms," Dakota said. "They would have given her a guest ID for the photo shoot."

"They didn't have those the last time I was here," Ivy said.

"Watch and learn, rookie," Dakota told her.

She took the ID badge she wore on a cord around her neck and swiped it through a slot next to a plain, metal door. There was a buzzing sound, and Dakota pushed the door open.

"So far, so good," she said. "Now we might start running into people. This isn't like thirty-two—people sometimes do stop you and ask what you're doing. Just look worried and walk fast. Don't make eye contact with people. They'll notice you less that way."

I would have no trouble looking worried. The thought of how much trouble we'd be in if we were caught made me feel sick. And if we got Ivy's mother in trouble . . . that I didn't even want to think about.

"Sounds like you've done some sneaking around before," I said, trying to reassure myself that Dakota and Ivy knew what we were doing.

"Of course," Dakota said. "How do you think I keep on top of all the gossip?"

"Let's just go," Ivy said.

Dakota pushed the door open and held it for us. We walked through into an unadorned hallway. Everything was beige: the floors, the walls, even the light fixtures. It had a generic, institutional feel that made it feel more like an old school than an office building. *City Nation* seemed to spare no expense glitzing up its appearance for the public. But here on the private floors, it was bare bones.

"Follow me," Dakota whispered. "See that water fountain down there? There's a doorway right after which leads into the junior designers' area. Just walk through it as fast as you can. Take your phones out and pretend to be texting. Don't look around."

"Okay," I said, and Ivy nodded.

We paused briefly at the doorway, then plunged in. Where the hallway had been pretty quiet, the design area was like a circus. People were snapping into phones, barking at each other. Two women were pushing a huge rack of clothes past a row of cubicles, trying not to bump into anyone's space. Someone was playing music, and in another cubicle was the sound of different music. I pulled out my phone and stared at it intently as I walked, typing an imaginary text to a fake person. Ivy was doing the same thing, and Dakota had her phone pressed to her ear, saying things like, "Yes, I can. When do you need them? And how many would you like?"

We'd gotten practically two-thirds of the way across the room toward the door at the opposite end.

This is working, I thought, typing another non-word on the phone. *We're going to make it.*

"Oh no. You are not supposed to be here," I heard a familiar voice say. My heart seemed to stop beating altogether. I didn't know many voices here, but I knew that one. It was unmistakably Garamond.

Don't react, I told myself. *He isn't talking to us. Just keep walking.*

"Dakota Whittier, Ivy Scanlon, and Paulina I've-forgotten-your-last-name, don't pretend you don't hear me."

Oh. Maybe he WAS talking to us.

We all stopped walking and turned toward Garamond. I felt a rush of panic and dropped my phone. It landed just a few feet from Garamond's shoes. I picked it up, keeping my eyes down. I could not look at him. I had no idea what to do, and I'm sure Ivy didn't, either.

"I'm sorry, what?" Dakota asked.

"Don't 'I'm sorry, what?' me, young lady," Garamond countered. "I'm in the middle of a crisis, as I'm sure you all know. I don't have time for this. You girls aren't supposed to be wandering around on this floor. What if Helvetica saw you?"

"She isn't in yet," Dakota said.

"That doesn't matter, Dakota. And, Ivy, you certainly shouldn't be here. I know you were all supposed to be at the shoot, but at the moment we don't *have* a shoot. You should all be in the interns' room where I left you."

"Well, I . . . we thought we were supposed to . . ." Dakota began.

"Garamond, we're looking for Quincy," Ivy said.

Garamond raised his eyebrows. "Darling, we're *all* looking for Quincy. If we don't find her soon, the photographer is going to walk, Helvetica's going to get back and find out we've misplaced our celebrity, and we're going to be in the middle of a big fat mess. I don't think *you* can help *us*."

"We had a couple of ideas of where she might have gone," Ivy pressed.

Garamond stared at Ivy for a moment, then his expression changed. "Oh, I see. You think she might have gone to the sample room. I can assure you, darling, that is the first place Constantia looked."

"But it can't hurt to have more people looking, can it?" Ivy said. "Maybe she didn't want Constantia to find her. Let's face it, Constantia isn't exactly the most approachable woman in the world."

Garamond sighed. "That may be true. But the point is, you aren't supposed to be on thirty-four unless you have a specific reason to be here. And this is the second time today, Ivy."

"The second time?" Ivy asked, confused. "What are you talking about?"

"Somebody told me they talked to you just a—" he said.

His phone rang again, and he hesitated a moment, looking at the screen.

"Oh, her again. Anyway, as I said, you know perfectly well you aren't supposed to be here." He looked thoughtful for a moment. "Though there is something to the idea that you might be better at figuring out what that girl is thinking than I am. And who knows—if you do find her, she may be more receptive to you than to me or Constantia. Okay, listen. We did not just have this conversation," he said. "Have your look-see, don't get caught, and get yourselves back where you're supposed to be. And if you happen upon Quincy, please tell her I've already fixed whatever it is she's unhappy about and get her to that studio!"

Then he whisked past us, answering his phone with a clipped, "Garamond speaking."

We stared at each other for a moment.

"I can't believe you told him what we were doing," Dakota said.

"Well, it worked, didn't it?" Ivy asked. "Mom would always bring me to his office to say hi when I visited. He likes me."

Which kind of meant that maybe he didn't like Dakota quite so much, and now she knew it, too.

"Um, shouldn't we go?" I asked. "We're still really not supposed to be here, right?"

"Follow me," Dakota said. "The sample room is down this way." She lead us past a rack hung with dresses, pants, and fake furs in every shade of red imaginable. A large note had been stuck to it that said FOR HELVETICA'S APPROVAL ONLY.

"Here it is."

We were standing outside an unmarked door painted battleship gray.

"What do we say to Quincy if she is here?" I asked.

"I have no idea," Dakota said, sliding her ID through the slot.

"What could we say that would convince her to go back to the shoot?" I pressed.

"You're supposed to be the think-on-your-feet girl," Dakota said, pushing the door open. "Just don't pick anything up. Everyone goes in for a look sooner or later. But if someone thinks you're taking something, that's a problem. Come on."

The first thing I noticed when I stepped into the sample room was the smell. It smelled like a department store times a hundred. I could make out leather and perfume and twenty other things my nose couldn't immediately identify.

There were small light fixtures set into the walls that cast a dim, amber-colored glow throughout the room. Dakota flicked a switch and turned on the overhead lights.

"Wow," I said.

When people talked about the sample room, I had imagined something small—a closet, really. This room was HUGE, with very high ceilings and racks and shelves and boxes everywhere. I didn't know where to look first. I could certainly see how someone could stay out of sight here if they wanted to. There were mannequins and deep racks of dresses and stacks of boxes somebody could duck behind.

To my right was a huge wall, maybe eighteen feet high and the length of two school buses, that was covered in shelves containing nothing but shoes. They seemed to be arranged in some semblance of order, with businesslike heels on the right, staggering glittery stilettos in the middle, and items in the boot family farther down the wall. It was a strange sight, and looking around the room, things just got weirder from there.

"Whoa," Ivy whispered. "I've only ever been in here once, and I was about eight. I thought it was creepy, and I never wanted to come back."

"It *is* kind of creepy," I said. "I feel like the shoes are looking at us. Wow! Look at those," I added, taking a few steps forward and pointing at a rack to our left where ball gown after ball gown hung, just waiting to be slipped on and swirled around the room. It was hard to pick out individual colors in the dim light, but I could see sequins and satin sheen and layers of tulle.

"There are other rooms," Dakota said. "See the handbag section there? There's a door next to it. That's coats. Over beyond the boots is another room for hats and scarves. I can't remember what the rest of them are. One of them is a whole little room just for lipstick."

"How are we going to—" I began, but Ivy silenced

me by pressing on my arm. She raised one finger in the air, indicating that we should listen.

After a moment, I heard it, too. A rustling sound in a short, quiet burst. Like the rustle of fabric against fabric.

Dakota pointed toward the room she'd said was for coats.

"That way," she said, walking toward the door. Ivy and I exchanged a quick look, then hurried after Dakota. We caught up with her just as she stepped through the doorway.

The room was lined with racks of every kind of coat I could imagine. Along the wall nearest to the door were a bunch of fur coats, all hanging together on a rod suspended from the ceiling. They made me think of Narnia—the fantasyland that lay on the other side of some coats just like these.

I was about to say that the room appeared to be empty when, suddenly, a rack of long winter wool jackets seemed to wobble. A hand emerged from between two sleeves, followed by a person.

"I was afraid you were that Constantia person," the girl said. "She's like a platoon sergeant with lipstick."

The girl had reddish hair that hung perfectly straight at chin level and small, pointy features. She wore leggings, a long tailored jacket, and a fat purple scarf wrapped several times around her neck. She wore no makeup and didn't look much older than me. She was fresh-faced and very pretty. If I hadn't spent the last hour talking about her, I would never have recognized her. But there was no mistaking it. This was definitely Quincy Vanderstan. I couldn't believe how casual she was being.

"I'm Paulina," I said. "This is Dakota, and that's Ivy."

Ivy smiled and gave a little wave. Dakota was absolutely frozen. She didn't seem to be able to move. *Self-assured Dakota is starstruck*, I thought.

"Ivy?" the girl asked. "One of the four magazine girls?"

Looking mystified, Ivy nodded.

"Garamond mentioned you this morning. Something about you coming up to the shoot with four questions. I love the name Ivy, so it kind of stuck with me. Someone stopped me on my way here, and I told them I was you. Sorry—hope I didn't get you into trouble. I needed to blow off some steam for a while."

"Uh, no problem," Ivy said.

That explains why Garamond thought Ivy had already been on thirty-four, I thought. How did Quincy manage to look so normal—so totally unrecognizable?

"I guess everyone's looking for me," Quincy said.

"Yes, they are," I said. "We were looking for you, too."

"Oh, I can be such an idiot," Quincy said, walking over to the rack of fur coats and running her hand along them. "It wasn't even any of the people here I was mad at—it was my mother."

"What happened?" Ivy asked. "Not that it's any of my business, but . . ."

"Oh please, I made it the whole magazine's business by leaving the shoot," Quincy said. "Garamond, who is a sweetheart by the way, was going over some ideas for what I should be wearing for the shoot, and he started showing me the coolest steampunk dresses he'd pulled when my mother interrupted him and said no, I need to have a more timeless, sophisticated look. She wanted me in Chanel or Halston, not that she could pick either of them out of a lineup. I'm eighteen years old, and my mother is standing there talking over my head, telling somebody what I have to wear. I had a long flight last night, and I had to get up way too early this morning, and I was cranky. I just blew my top. My mother snapped at me and got all angry, and when everyone was running around pulling gowns for her to look at, I just slipped out."

Dakota blinked a few times, like she'd just awakened in her own body.

"Steampunk? Do you mean the Violetta collection?" she asked.

"Yeah!" Quincy said. "They were Violetta. How did you know?"

Dakota visibly relaxed, obviously relieved that she had found the power of speech again.

"I'm an intern here. I got to sit in when they were laying out the article about her Milan collection," Dakota said.

"Oh, I was actually at that show," Quincy said. "That's what got me into steampunk in the first place. My mother hates it, naturally. So here I am. Constantia came in here looking for me before, and I just couldn't face her. She's so . . . proper. So I ducked into the coatrack until she left. Did everyone go ballistic?"

"Oh, they're all frantic," Dakota said cheerfully. "The whole building is talking about it."

Good one, Dakota, I thought as Quincy covered her face with her hands. "Oh no," she groaned. "This has all happened so fast. A year ago I was just a high school kid with a part in a TV show. Then it was like one morning I had a movie, and then another movie, and suddenly I'm in the spotlight all the time. It sounds great, and a lot of the time it is. But sometimes you don't want the entire world to be watching you. I acted like such a baby and messed up

119

the whole shoot. How can I go back and face them?"

"Actually, Quincy, it doesn't really become a problem until Helvetica Grenier gets to the office," I explained.

"Exactly," Ivy said. "My mom says shoots run late all the time, for any number of reasons. They expect that, it's normal. What they're worried about is Helvetica showing up and asking where you are, and nobody being able to tell her."

Quincy looked up. "And she isn't in the building yet?"

"No," I said. "Listen, you could have taken off for any number of reasons. For all anyone knows, you . . . you saw a mouse or something. It wouldn't be the first time. We could all just go back up there together and walk in as a group. Believe me, nobody will care *why* you left. All they want is to have you back so they can get on with the shoot."

"Absolutely," Ivy said. "We'll all walk in together. Nobody will be anything less than thrilled. And Helvetica will never know. Believe me, no one is going to tell her they lost a movie star!"

"Really? Oh I can definitely do that, going in as a group," Quincy said. "You guys are great."

Dakota's phone made a little chirping sound, and she held it in front her.

"Well, it might be too late to slip in unnoticed," she

120

said. "Whit just texted that Helvetica's on her way up in the elevator right now."

"Oh no," Quincy said. "I can't face her like this. It's too humiliating. Once Helvetica finds out how unprofessional I was, everyone in the whole industry will know."

"No, they won't," Ivy said firmly. "First of all, Helvetica can be a terror to work for, but she keeps what goes on at *City Nation* very quiet. My mom has told me that more than once. Second, it's not necessarily too late. Dakota, did Whit say Helvetica was on her way up to the studio or just that she was on her way up?"

Dakota checked the text again. "Just that she was on her way up," she said.

"So if she just got here from her meeting, wouldn't she go to her office first?" Ivy asked.

"Yeah, she would!" Dakota said. "She'll go to her office to put away her coat and have a fresh coffee. Nobody is allowed to disturb her until she's had that coffee. Then she calls Constantia in to get the morning roundup. She always does it that way, every single time."

"But if we take the elevator, we might run into her," Quincy said. "You know what? I'll just have to risk it. I created this mess in the first place. The least I can do is own it."

"No, you don't have to," Dakota said. "There's a way to get to the studio from here that I can guarantee Helvetica won't be taking."

That seemed like a difficult promise to keep, but Quincy immediately brightened.

"Cool! Let's go!" she said.

We dashed to the door, Ivy stopping long enough to switch off the lights. "Where are we going?" she asked Dakota, who was heading down the opposite direction from the elevators.

"Fire stairs," she said. "You aren't supposed to be able to get from the stairwell back onto a floor. But people always prop the doors open so they can go between floors without going out to the elevators. It's so much faster. This way."

She pulled open a door, but not before I read a sign on it that said FIRE DOOR—NO REENTRY. I hoped she knew what she was talking about. From what I'd seen of Dakota, chances were she did, but now that Helvetica was in the office, we really had to stay hidden.

The sounds of our footsteps made clattering sounds that echoed up and down the stairwell. I couldn't believe Dakota could climbs stairs that fast in the shoes she had on.

"Hey, Quincy," said Ivy, sounding a little out of breath. "How did you even know where the sample room was? There's no sign on it or anything."

"Hah. I was wondering when one of you was going to ask me that. It's because this isn't my first time visiting *City Nation*," Quincy said cheerfully as we rounded a landing and started up another flight. "About a year ago I was picked to be in the 'Young Up-and-Coming' layout. You know that huge picture they do every year with the forty actors under age twenty-five they think are most likely to make it big?"

"Oh, with the foldout picture? I love it when they do that!" I said. "You were in one of those?"

"Yep!" Quincy said. "And they gave us a tour. It's all a blur, except for the sample room. We just kind of peeked in, then we had to go. I told myself that day if I ever found myself at *City Nation* again, which I was positive I wouldn't, that I would get a better look at the sample room. And when I got my chance, I remembered more or less where it was. And the guest pass they gave me unlocked the door."

"That's amazing!" Ivy said. "One year later, and you're going to be on the cover!"

"I know—it doesn't seem real," Quincy said. "Sometimes I still think it's all just a really cool dream."

"It's open!" Dakota was exclaiming. She had reached the next landing and was holding open a door. "Didn't I tell you?"

"You did," Ivy said. "I'm not sure even Constantia knows as much about how this place runs as you do. Good work."

I smiled at my friend. Whether Ivy liked someone or not, she always made a point of giving credit where it was due. It was one of the many things I really liked about her.

Directly through the door was a little alcove with shelves stacked with bottles of water and a small refrigerator and microwave on a makeshift countertop. A heavy black curtain covered a space to our left, and light streamed in behind it.

"How do we get to the studio?" I asked.

"We're in it," Dakota said. "Follow me." Then she ducked around the black curtain.

Ivy pulled one corner of the curtain to the side, and together we walked through.

· chapter ·
11

We were in a large, high-ceilinged room with enormous windows. At one end of the room was a white screen surrounded by large electric lights, several fans, and a bank of computers. On another wall were rack after rack of dresses, and near that were three tables covered with makeup. A group of people were standing together near the computers. More than half of them were dressed entirely in black, and all of them were talking on their cell phones.

I felt like Dorothy and her friends arriving at the palace of the Great and Terrible Oz. We'd come all this way, and for a moment nothing was happening. No one seemed to realize we had arrived. Then a slim older woman with a mass of curly gray hair tucked partly under a black newsboy cap turned and caught sight of us.

"Quincy!" she exclaimed.

And then EVERYONE was looking at us, and people were popping out from behind screens, around doorways—they seemed to be appearing out of thin air from every conceivable direction, several of them uttering an astonished "Quincy!" as they did. I saw Vicky looking around, trying to spot Quincy, while Bob switched on his camera.

In just moments, a crowd of editors, stylists, photographers, and assistants were surrounding Quincy without actually getting all that close to her. *She won't be escaping a second time today*, I thought.

"You crazy, brilliant girls—I can't believe you did it!"

Garamond was standing with Ivy's mother, looking from us to Quincy with an expression of utter delight. He bounded over to us and enveloped Ivy in a hug.

"What am I missing?" Mrs. Scanlon asked. "Garamond, what did they do? Whatever it is, I think I'm extremely happy about it."

"Dakota came in and told us what was going on," Ivy said. "We got to talking, and we tried to figure out where Quincy would have gone. Then Dakota and Miko came up with an idea, and we went to check it out."

"And you found her!" Garamond said. "I want to

know everything. Every detail! But not right now."

He turned and pushed his way through the people surrounding Quincy.

"Quincy, darling!" I heard him say. "I was just this second wondering where you were. Are you ready for makeup?"

Mrs. Scanlon shook her head in amazement, smiling at us. "And just like that, the shoot is back on," she said. "This really is a crazy place, and you girls seem to fit right in. Listen, however you managed this— and Garamond isn't the only one who wants to hear every single detail—you've saved the day. Text Tally and Miko and tell them how to get up here, okay? I'll get word to the receptionist to let them through. You four have definitely earned the right to cover this shoot!"

"Thanks, Mom," Ivy said, her face shining.

"What about me?" Dakota asked.

Mrs. Scanlon hesitated. "Oh dear. Technically I don't have the authority to allow an intern on set. That's really Garamond's call," she said. "But none of us are going to be able to get within three feet of him until this shoot is over."

"Mom, we couldn't have even found Quincy without Dakota," Ivy said. "If there's any way it's possible, she deserves to be here more than we do."

Dakota stared at Ivy in astonishment, like she just

couldn't believe Ivy had just spoken up for her like that. How could Dakota have known Ivy for so many years and not have realized what an AWESOME girl she was? And more than that, what an AMAZING friend.

"It's true," I said. "Dakota was the mastermind."

"Then I owe you a big thanks as well, Dakota," Mrs. Scanlon said. "And by all means, please stay. I'm sure Garamond will agree. Eventually."

There was a bit of a commotion, and heads began turning.

"Is it Helvetica?" Ivy whispered, standing on the tips of her toes to try and see over all the people between us and the studio's main entrance.

I got a quick glimpse and nodded. Helvetica Grenier had arrived.

She wasn't the tallest person in New York, but every person in that room instantly registered her presence. You could practically feel the moment when everyone became super self-conscious. Helvetica was talking to Constantia and scanning the room with narrowed, thoughtful eyes. She was dressed head to toe in red.

"Wow, red!" I murmured even though I knew you weren't supposed to comment.

"It's Etruscan Pomegranate," someone near me corrected softly.

Of course it was. I checked just to make sure I

wasn't wearing Etruscan Pomegranate. My sweater was definitely Flamingo Pink. I was safe.

"There's room for all of us to sit on the windowsill," Dakota said. "We'll be able to see everything from there."

"Great," Ivy said. "Miko says they're on their way up!"

Dakota was right again. From our vantage point on the wide, sunny window ledge, we could see almost everything that was going on in the room.

The gray-haired woman in the newsboy cap and an oversize mountain of a man in a shiny green jacket had wheeled a rack to the center of the room, where Garamond stood inspecting it. He pointed at a dress and then another and then a third. The woman removed the three dresses from the rack and carried them to a curtained-off area in the corner that might have been a changing area.

"Those are Violettas," Dakota remarked. "Looks like Quincy is getting what she wanted after all."

"Oh! There's Tally and Miko!" I said, waving both my hands in the air to get their attention. Ivy did the same. Miko caught sight of us right away and led Tally by the arm over to us. Tally was looking from right to left, her eyes wide, taking everything in. I noticed with a laugh that she had one hand pressed over her mouth. Tally was going to do whatever it took to keep herself out of the spotlight at *City Nation*.

"What happened?" Miko asked when she reached us. "You guys never came back. So we figured someone found Quincy."

I grinned. "WE found Quincy," I said.

Tally pulled her hand away from her face. "You did?" she exclaimed.

"She was in the sample room, just like we thought, Miko," Dakota said.

"Wait, rewind," Miko said. "Tell us exactly what happened after you left the interns' office."

"Quiet, please!" I heard Garamond bellow. I was amazed that he had such a huge voice. The entire room instantly fell silent.

"Thank you. We are ready to go," Garamond announced. "If you do not have specific authorization to be here, now is the time to leave. This is a closed set. If you don't know if you're supposed to be here, then you're *not* supposed to be here. Everyone else, I'm very pleased to present the beautiful and very talented Quincy Vanderstan, wearing Violetta."

Quincy emerged from behind the curtained area with a brilliant smile on her face. She was wearing an eggplant-purple tea-length dress that looked classically old, maybe Victorian, with a plaid jacket that was short and tailored and fitted together with tiny gear-shaped links. The dress flowed fully in multiple, slightly off-kilter layers, and the whole outfit was crowned by a shiny black top hat, over which was fitted a pair of gleaming metal and glass goggles.

"Wow!" Ivy said. "She looks amazing!"

Everyone began to clap. Bob had the camera trained on Quincy, who beamed at everyone happily. When she caught sight of us on the window ledge, she waved. Bob turned the camera toward us, and for a moment I felt self-conscious, but then I waved back at Quincy. She looked so happy!

"Before we begin," Garamond continued, "Helvetica would like to say something."

Helvetica tucked one perfect lock of hair behind her ear to reveal an exquisite Etruscan Pomegranate earring.

"Not much more than a year ago, we selected forty young actors and actresses for our annual 'Young Up-and-Coming' photo spread," Helvetica said. "I'm therefore not just pleased, but proud, that one of those actresses will be featured on our December cover. She has accomplished an extraordinary amount this year, and I'm certain this is just the beginning. I know you'll all agree when I say that Quincy Vanderstan is a most outstanding young lady. She's beautiful, she's talented, and though very young, she is already a complete professional and a pleasure to work with. We're very honored, Quincy, to have you here today."

Everyone clapped again, and Bob pointed the camera at Helvetica, taking several steps toward her. Vicky appeared behind him, and she moved toward Helvetica, too. A ripple went through the room, and I made a little gasp as I realized what was going on.

Vicky was wearing red. All red. A deep, vibrant red almost the precise shade of . . . well . . . Etruscan Pomegranate.

Helvetica walked forward several feet, enough so that Vicky was no longer in her line of sight. I saw two people converge on the TV producer and lead her, protesting and confused, from the room.

"I would not have believed that if I hadn't seen it with my own eyes," I murmured.

"Before I leave you to your work," Helvetica continued, "I'd like to extend one other welcome. We're very pleased to be hosting a visit from four young publishers. Paulina Barbosa, Miko Suzuki, Tally Janeway, and Ivy Scanlon—daughter of our own Karen—who write, design, and publish their own magazine for girls. I am very happy to have the chance to encourage and endorse *4 Girls* magazine. These girls are the future of our industry both as readers and publishers. If they are any indication of what's to come, our future is bright indeed."

For just a few seconds, everyone in the room was looking at the four of us. We had been recognized, we had been appreciated, and we had been praised. By Helvetica Grenier.

What a story that would make!

· chapter ·

12

Bright lights had been switched on, and the photo shoot finally seemed to be starting, but Quincy said something to Garamond, then rushed over to where we were sitting.

"I just had to come over for a second! How cool was that shout-out Helvetica gave you?" she asked. "Are you dying?"

A makeup person had followed Quincy and was hovering around her with a little brush, adding some final touches.

"We couldn't believe it. And you look gorgeous!" Ivy said.

"Quincy, this is Miko and Tally, the other half of *4 Girls*," I said.

"Hi," Miko said a little shyly.

"I'm not supposed to talk too much because I do that a lot, but I just *love* you, and I've seen every *single* thing you've done. I mean, not that you've *ever* done, but on TV and in the movies done," Tally said in one breath, shaking Quincy's hand energetically.

"That's so sweet!" Quincy said. "Okay, I've got to go before Garamond comes after me. Just wanted to thank you guys again. Did you hear Helvetica called me professional and a pleasure to work with? And did you see?" she called over her shoulder. "Got my steampunk!"

"I can't believe I just met Quincy Vanderstan," Miko said. "And what a dress!"

"What exactly *is* steampunk?" I asked.

"It's like, imagine what things would look like in the 1800s if the future had come faster. Picture Victorian styles mixed with sort of high technology incorporated into the design. Only the technology has to look like it was made in Victorian times, too."

"Oh," I said. I still wasn't sure I really got it, but now I knew it looked supercool.

The tallest, thinnest man I'd ever seen was showing Quincy where to stand on the set as another woman fussed with her hair.

"Wow, that's Raavi, the photographer," Miko said. "He's not even thirty yet, and he's done so many cover shoots. I'm a huge fan of his work."

"You should tell him that after the shoot," Ivy

said. "Garamond might be able to introduce you. He totally loves you."

"He will? He does?" Miko asked excitedly. Ivy nodded. Dakota folded her arms and stared straight ahead. Apparently Miko was the competition now.

"Hey, we're missing our story here," said Ivy. "One of us should record an intro before they start shooting. We're actually here as this is happening. Let's share that with our readers."

"Oh, right, I'm sorry," Miko said, fumbling with her little camera. "Who wants to do the intro? Tally?"

"Yes!" Tally said instantly.

"Better hurry, guys," I said. Raavi had walked over to his camera, and Quincy was standing expectantly on the set, waiting for his instructions.

"Maybe stand here, so we can get them setting up the shot in the background," Miko said, pointing the camera at Tally. "Let's give it a try. Ready?"

"Ready," Tally said. And before my eyes, Tally morphed from a giddy girl into a put-together, seasoned reporter.

"*4 Girls* is thrilled to be reporting to our readers from inside the famous photo studio at *City Nation* magazine, where legendary, iconic photographer Raavi is about to begin shooting the December cover. We told you we'd let you know who the mystery celebrity is, and now we can! *4 Girls* is thrilled to introduce you to one of the hottest actresses in Hollywood . . . Quincy Vanderstan!"

Tally is so great at this, I thought. *She just gets better and better on camera.*

"When you see *City Nation*, you probably have no idea about the incredible amount of work that goes into a single photograph. Behind this shoot are teams of professionals: photographers, lighting specialists, editors, makeup artists, and stylists. They all work together long before the shoot starts to determine exactly what the photos should look and feel like, what clothes will be worn, what story will be told."

Wow. How did Tally suddenly know all this stuff?

"In the age of digital photography, Raavi will be able to have instant feedback on his photos at the computer. If he doesn't like the way something looks, he can change it immediately. No more waiting for prints to come back and scouring them with a magnifying glass!

"Quincy will be here anywhere from two to five hours or more, depending on how things go. All of these jobs, from the photographer to the design director to Quincy herself seem so glamorous! But this is where all the exhausting work comes in. And if they do it right, *City Nation*'s readers will never know about the incredible effort it took!"

Tally took a breath and stepped forward.

"How was that?" she whispered.

Ivy and I stared at her, amazed. "That was fabulous," I said. "But . . . how did you know all that stuff?"

"What do you think she was doing all this time trapped with me and Whit in the interns' office?" Miko said with a grin. "She's been grilling poor Whit and anybody else she could grab. You've never heard anyone ask so many questions in under an hour. And Whit really knows his stuff! We got a lot of great information—enough to use even if we didn't end up getting to be at the photo shoot. But here we are!"

"Okay, everybody. Quiet on set, please!" Raavi shouted.

Quincy walked to the center of the room. Two guys instantly moved forward holding things that looked like shields, which reflected the light to make Quincy look brighter. Miko pointed the camera and began to film.

"A little more," Raavi said. The guys moved closer as Raavi held a little computerized machine out.

"He's measuring the light," Dakota explained.

"Okay, gorgeous, you ready?" Raavi asked.

Quincy gave him a brilliant smile. "Absolutely," she replied.

Raavi positioned his camera in front of something that looked like a massive satellite dish.

"Go ahead and look down," Raavi called, and began shooting pictures. "Chin up slightly, eyes over my shoulder, please. More lively, livelier, gorgeous. Yes, that's perfect!"

As we watched in silence, Raavi barked out a series of commands that Quincy seemed to follow effortlessly. He had her sit, stand, whirl around, and jump in the air. Someone produced a tiny, fluffy dog on a leash that they wanted her to hold, which I didn't realize was real until it sneezed. Then they took the dog away, gave her a set of jacks and a rubber ball, and had her lie on her stomach and play. By the time Raavi was done, I was totally exhausted, and I hadn't done anything but watch!

When Raavi went to peer at the images displayed on the computer, surrounded by three identical-looking helpers, someone dashed onto the set and handed Quincy a bottle of water and touched up her hair and makeup.

"Okay, we've got it!" Raavi called. "Next dress, please."

Next dress? They did all this with more than one outfit? But of course they did. This was a major photo spread for a top-notch magazine.

Tally and Miko were already set up again.

"So what you can get an idea of here is that for one photograph, that took about an hour of work just to

139

get Quincy styled, adjust the lights, and get a good picture. Keep in mind that of the hundreds of shots they'll be going for, you might see only half in the magazine. These people work hard!" Tally declared.

Quincy had been ushered into the changing area.

"We're getting some really good stuff here," Ivy said, shaking her head. "It's all happening so fast. Tal, what do you think about maybe trying to get a quick interview with someone. Maybe one of Raavi's assistants? Just a few questions about—"

"Got it!" Tally said. She rushed off toward a short, red-haired girl in black jeans and a black and purple shirt who didn't look much older than Quincy. Ivy and I inched forward a little to listen.

"Hi, I'm Tally Janeway from *4 Girls* magazine," Tally said.

The girl's face lit up. "Oh, the one Helvetica was talking about," she said.

Helvetica had done us a huge favor giving us a public shout-out like that. Now everybody was treating us like we were the real deal.

"That's right! Can you tell us about yourself—your name and job title and what that means in real life?"

The girl looked over at Raavi, who was deep in a heated discussion with Garamond. They were both pointing at either the computer or the guy running the computer.

"Sure, I think I have a few minutes," she said, looking into the camera Miko had trained on her. "My name is Kristen. I'm one of Raavi's junior assistants. He's got, like, seven assistants total."

"And what does a junior assistant do?" Tally asked.

The girl laughed. "Well, it'd be easier to tell you what I *don't* do. Basically the answer is anything Raavi needs. I might be getting coffee or running down to the sample room to pull a dress in a different color. Sometimes I do the light readings or run interference with editorial if there's a problem. If we're going to an outside shoot, I check the site in advance to make sure everything is working right and is going to mesh with Raavi's equipment. Sometimes he even has me be the stand-in if the model gets tired. I literally never know what I'll be doing next."

"But do you like it? Is it fun?" Tally pressed.

"Oh, it's amazing!" Kristen said. "It doesn't pay much, but Raavi is superfamous. I'm lucky to have the chance to watch him work at all. I'm learning so, so much. The hours can be really long and hard, especially if we're doing a shoot somewhere outside where it's hot or cold. We went to this elephant rescue place last year, and I almost had sunstroke. But I wouldn't trade this job for the world. One day, I'll be running a shoot like this!"

"Oh, you will, I'm sure of it!" Tally said. "And then we'll be able to look back and say we interviewed you for *4 Girls* before you were famous!"

"Okay, let's go people. Time is money!" Raavi called, clapping his hands together.

Quincy came out from the changing area, completely transformed. She was wearing a red plaid gown with an elaborate black corset stitched over it. The back of the corset was hand-stitched in a design that looked like it was an X-ray of her spine. The corset was clasped together with tiny keys. The front of her skirt was tied up to reveal knee-high lace-up boots that looked like regular boots from the front, but from the back were held together by a skeleton of metal tabs and wires. She looked like something straight out of a sci-fi novel.

"Gorgeous!" Raavi said. "Someone get the dog again, please? Okay, let's go!"

And they started all over again, Raavi calling out his instructions and Quincy complying, like an Olympic-level game of Simon Says. And when that one was done, Quincy changed into a third dress, and they were back to square one.

It was almost four o'clock when Raavi announced that they were done.

"Can you believe that took more than four hours?" Ivy whispered to me.

"Yes and no," I said. "It was like forever, but I feel like we just got here!"

"Wait!" Quincy called. "There's one more thing we need to do."

Raavi frowned and walked over to her. They spoke for several moments, then Raavi nodded.

"*4 Girls*, front and center, please," he called.

What?

Ivy was already walking toward Ravi, Miko close behind fiddling with the camera.

"Quincy would like a shot with you all," he said.

My mouth dropped open. Me? *Us?* In a Raavi picture with a movie star?

But there was no time to protest or worry about what I looked like or do anything but be as instantly obedient as Quincy had been. The four of us joined Quincy on the set. Though there was a blast of icy air coming from the vent overhead, I was amazed at how hot and disorienting it was under the lights. How had Quincy posed for four hours?

"Okay, Quincy here, then you here, uh, Miko, is it? And curly blond hair here, and big eyes, you stand on the other side."

Apparently I was big eyes. I stood next to Quincy, and Miko, Tally, and Ivy were on her other side. My eyes were getting used to the lights, and I could see a little better now. Miko had kept the camera on

143

and was actually filming the whole thing from our perspective. I saw Ivy's mother walking toward us.

"Ready?" Raavi asked.

"Wait. You should hold this," Mrs. Scanlon said, stepping up onto the little platform and holding something out in her hand.

"Oh, your magazine!" Quincy exclaimed, taking it. She held it, cover facing out, and smiled.

"We're ready, Raavi," she called.

I was NOT ready. I was so nervous I thought I was going to throw up. Quincy was a pro, Tally loved this stuff, Miko was amazing at keeping cool, and Ivy had such a glow of happiness about her there was no way she was going to take a bad photo. But me, I was a ball of nerves.

"Let me see lively! Let me see *4 Girls* at work! Let me see each of you, as you really are, right here!" Raavi called out.

I had time to think what a funny direction that was to give someone, to suddenly start acting like herself. I started to smile a little, and I heard Tally make a classic Tally squeal, and I felt Quincy squeeze my arm.

Then it was over.

"Got it!" Raavi announced. "Okay, that's a wrap! Thanks, everyone!"

And suddenly everyone was putting things away,

lights were being switched off, and people were filing out the door. Garamond whooshed by, pushing the rack of Violetta dresses, and Constantia whisked Quincy away, but not before she grabbed Mrs. Scanlon by the arm and said something that made Ivy's mom nod and smile.

"Oh, there she goes," Tally said. Constantia had ushered Quincy to the door, where a serious-looking woman was waiting. "We didn't get to say good-bye."

"Hey, the picture was a nice surprise, huh?" Mrs. Scanlon asked.

"I can't believe you had a copy of *4 Girls* to hand Quincy," I said to Mrs. Scanlon. "That was so great of you. The picture is going to be priceless!"

"Are you kidding? I've been carrying it around with me everywhere to show people," she said. "What a day, huh? Unfortunately, we've run so late I'm afraid you've missed the chance to go through the storyboarding process. They'll be finishing up very soon, and I still have to be here for a while."

"It's okay. I think we've got more than enough material," Ivy said.

"Good, I'm glad you're not disappointed," Mrs. Scanlon told us. "We'll still have tomorrow morning for you to watch them post all the photographs then go through the process of picking which ones to use. And we'll have the afternoon for sightseeing. And . . . I have one more thing to tell you."

"More?" Tally said.

"Quincy has a live appearance booked on *Letterman*, and she's going to have to rush off to get there in time. She's not going to be able to stick around for your questions right now, but she offered a compromise that I think you guys are going to like. Quincy's got a few hours free tomorrow, and when we're done here, she'd like all of you to go with her for a limousine tour of Manhattan. Think you'd like to do that?"

Like to?

"Yes!" all four of us said at the same time.

Mrs. Scanlon laughed. "Thought so," she said. "Okay, sit tight, and I'll come and get you when it's time to go."

It didn't seem possible, but our trip seemed to just keep getting better and BETTER.

· chapter ·
13

The four of us stood in the corner, trying to stay out of the way. Helvetica, Garamond, and the gray-haired woman from the photo shoot were standing shoulder to shoulder, staring at a backlit wall where rows of photographs of Quincy had been stuck on display like X-rays.

"The morning is half gone already. Let's speed this up. What's going on here, Georgia?" Helvetica asked, pointing at a photograph of Quincy wearing a long green gown and blowing bubbles through a little plastic ring. "And why this color?"

Helvetica was wearing loose-fitting pants and a silk shirt of deep green, or rather, as we had learned on our way up in the elevator, Brasilia Viridian.

"I've juxtaposed the Halston gown, which is obviously a look more suited for an older woman, with the pink bubble ring. I wanted to capture the essence of a child playing dress-up. An actress taking on a part but remaining authentic to herself. The bubbles she's blowing are her hopes, her playfulness. I love it," Georgia said.

"It's not working," Helvetica said briskly, and Garamond reached over and pulled the picture down.

"Okay, next is the Chanel," Garamond said, pointing to a picture of Quincy in an elegant pink suit, holding a dog.

"Why is she in Chanel to start with?" Helvetica asked. "She's eighteen years old. Why not a more youthful designer? It's not her."

"Her manager was pushing a classic look for some of the shots," Georgia said. "She doesn't want Quincy to be typecast as the sci-fi sidekick—she wants more directors to consider her for serious features."

My feet were killing me, but there was nowhere for me to sit. There wasn't even anything to lean against. I shifted from one foot to another as quietly as I could. Garamond had let us know we couldn't take photographs or video during this meeting, so I was taking as many notes as I could. But I had to hold my pad out in the air in front of me to write, and my arms were starting to hurt.

"Not our problem. First of all the manager is her mother," Helvetica said. "She has no idea what she's doing. Quincy needs to get herself a professional manager now that her career has taken off. Anyway, Georgia, you're the creative director. I want to know what you think. Why am I looking at this picture?"

"Quincy is very young and fresh-faced, but she's also got a classic profile," Georgia said. "In some of these pictures she looks like a real classic beauty. Jackie O., Audrey Hepburn. But the pink is playful, girlish. I think it works."

"I don't. Lose it," Helvetica commanded. Garamond pulled the picture down, and Georgia sighed quietly.

I nudged Ivy, who gave me a look that said "Aren't you glad you don't work for her?"

"Moving on," Helvetica said. "This is an eight-page spread, and we've still got too many looks. What is going on with this Violetta thing? Why are three of Quincy's looks by the same designer?"

"Quincy specifically requested to wear Violetta," Garamond said.

"Fine, so we keep one, maybe two. Why three?"

"Well, I was envisioning that as the signature look," Georgia said, pulling her gray curly hair into a ponytail, then letting it spring free again. "That's why I want to use one of the Violetta shots for the cover."

"You're going to have to do a better job than that talking me into it," Helvetica said. "I know Quincy likes the look. I like her in it. But as a cover statement, what are you trying to do? Who is going to respond to this?"

"Me," Miko murmured.

Helvetica whirled around, and the entire world seemed to stand still. "What? Please, one of you said something, and I'd like to hear it," Helvetica said.

Miko glanced at Garamond, who nodded, though he looked nervous. Georgia seemed happy to be out of the hot seat for the moment.

"Well, I was thinking about who's going to buy this issue, and why," Miko said. "At breakfast, Ivy's mom was explaining to us about the . . . what was the word, Ivy?"

"Demographics," Ivy said. "Thinking in advance about what age group you're going to most appeal to and whether they are mostly male or female. How much money they spend. Things like that."

"Right, so with Quincy Vanderstan on your cover, you already know her fan base is pretty young, with not all that much money," Miko explained. "Quincy has been on a bunch of covers recently. You see her face everywhere. So just the fact that she's on *City Nation*'s cover might not convince me to buy *this* particular magazine. But Quincy wearing Violetta, now that really catches my eye. For the people who are into fashion, they're going to recognize the steampunk look and want to see more. But even for people who don't know it, there's so much going on with this look. It's really young and edgy, but it also has this element of history in it that catches your attention, and then all the tech details make it look futuristic. So somebody who likes Quincy might not necessarily buy this magazine when she's in so many other ones right now. But a magazine like *City Nation* putting Quincy in this look, that is definitely something I'm going to spend my money on because I feel like I'm going to get a serious fashion experience, too, not just a *Life & Style* type interview with some pretty pictures. I can't speak for your older readers, but I can tell you how girls my age would respond."

Miko finished, and there was a long silence. Helvetica was looking thoughtfully at Miko. Georgia looked surprised, and Garamond was nervously rolling up his tie, then letting it unroll.

"Miko's hit on something key here," Helvetica said. "Not just because of her very good assessment of the Violetta look, but because she's given me an interesting perspective on why a young person might choose to buy this particular issue, this particular cover. Of all our readers, the youngest ones are the most likely to choose the Internet over buying a printed magazine. We need to be consistently coming up with ways to get them back and cultivate new readers. Okay, I'm convinced. We'll keep all three

Violetta looks and use one for the cover."

Garamond nodded and made a note. He acted very casual, like this was all no big deal, but when Helvetica leaned forward to get a better look at the picture Georgia had chosen for the cover, he turned around and blew a kiss at Miko.

I gave her an admiring glance. I had felt pretty certain the four of us would hold our own at *City Nation*, and we had. But Miko had gone far beyond that. She seemed to be thinking and contributing on a professional level. *She could really do this*, I thought. *She could be another Garamond. Maybe even another Helvetica. She was* THAT *good.*

"And I like this one for the cover because its irreverent," Georgia was saying. "The way Quincy's kicking one foot in the air and the dog's tongue is coming out just a little like it's going to kiss her. The top hat is very severe, but the energy is giddy."

Helvetica stared at the picture for several moments. Garamond and Georgia both seemed to be holding their breath.

"Yes," Helvetica said. "I love it. Okay, we're done. Garamond, I'll need to see the layout by three."

She started to leave, then came partway back in the door and looked at the four of us.

"Oh. This is your last meeting with us, isn't it?" she asked.

"Yes," Ivy said. "You've been so incredibly generous. You can't imagine what this experience has meant to us. I know we're here because my mom asked, but—"

"You're here because your mother showed me your magazine," Helvetica corrected. "Believe me, if I opened up *City Nation* every time one of my people asked, I'd be overrun. I like the way you girls think, and *4 Girls* speaks for itself. Miko has just given me some absolutely professional input, and I understand we are going with an idea Tally suggested in an editorial meeting. I think we benefited just as much from having you here as you did. You're welcome any time, all of you. Good luck."

"Thank you," I said in unison with Tally.

"Thank you *so* much," Miko added.

Helvetica nodded and swept off, the sound of her heels clacking on the floor echoing in the hallway.

"I still liked the Halston," Georgia said, sounding weary and heading for the door. "I'll be in my office, Garamond. Nice meeting you girls."

"What a morning," Garamond declared. "Let me walk out with you. Where is your mother meeting you?"

"We have to go back to the interns' office to get our coats," Ivy said.

"Then let me escort you to the elevator," Garamond

said. "It's probably the only fun I'll have all day. I've gotten used to you all now. What am I going to do without you? I could lose another movie star, and who will save me next time?"

"Oh, call us," Tally said. "We can save you over the phone!"

"I just might do that," Garamond said, chuckling. "Oh, I wish your mother still worked here full-time, Ivy. I really miss having her around."

"She still comes in once a week," Ivy said. "Plus, you could always come up and visit us."

"Oh, I hate leaving the city," Garamond said as we approached the elevator. "But for the Scanlons, I will consider it."

I reached out to push the up button, but Garamond gestured for me to wait.

"Darlings, you are all amazing, but Miko you really are a fashion miracle," Garamond said. "I want you to think about something. There are several summer internships at *City Nation*. One of them is in the design department. If you want it, it's yours. I know you're not local, so you'd have to figure something out. But don't say no—don't say anything right now. The competition for a *City Nation* summer internship is cutthroat. It's a major opportunity. If you're serious about getting into design, Miko, then find a way to make it work. You're good enough, no question, but so are a thousand other girls. E-mail me, and I'll tell you more about it."

He pushed the button. The elevator must have already been there because the doors opened immediately.

"And here we are. Have a safe trip home, girls. Remember, Miko, I want to hear from you. Good-bye, darlings!"

"Good-bye," I said, sad to see Garamond disappear as the doors slid shut. I was really starting to like him.

"Miko," Ivy said, grabbing her by both arms. "You do realize how huge this is, right? Garamond's serious. People would kill for a summer internship in design."

"My head is spinning," Miko said. "I don't know what to think. My parents want me to audition for a violin program this summer at the Music Conservatory. I don't know how I could possibly convince them to let me do this."

"My mom could talk to them," Ivy said. "She could show them what a once-in-a-lifetime chance this is."

"Would she do that?" Miko asked.

"Are you kidding? Of course she would," Ivy told her. "It can't hurt to try, right? You never know what could happen."

Whit and Dakota were both sitting at their desks

talking to each other when we got to the interns'
office. Whit stood up as we came in.

"Oh, good, I didn't miss you!" he said. "I'm due on
thirty-four to help with the filing, but I was hoping
I'd get to see you guys before you took off."

"We just helped pick the cover!" Tally exclaimed.

"Oh, please," Dakota said. "You're here for three
days, and already you think you're doing Georgia's
job? Get over yourselves."

I wanted to be nice to Dakota, but I hated the
way she always tried to put us down—even after Ivy
helped her stay at the photo shoot. I felt a surge of
competitiveness myself.

"Garamond offered the summer design internship
to Miko," I said.

Dakota's mouth dropped.

"Whoa," Whit said. "Congratulations! That's
major."

"I don't know if I can do it," Miko said. "It would
be really complicated. But I'm going to try my hardest
to work it out."

"I'm going for the editorial internship," Dakota
announced. "That's the *really* important one."

"You should go for that, too, Ivy," Whit said. "It
would be great to have you around this summer."

"Thanks for the vote of confidence, Whit," Dakota
said, looking angry.

"What?" Whit asked, looking confused. "Why does that have to mean I don't think you'd be great for it, too? You're both my friends, Dakota."

"Whatever," Dakota said, getting up. "I'm going to go get a soda." She darted out the door.

"Don't mind her," Whit said. "You know how she gets when she's feeling insecure."

"Insecure?" I asked. "She comes off as a lot of things, but insecure isn't one of them."

"It's all an act," Whit told me. "You should go for that internship, Ivy. Don't stay away just because of Dakota. It would be awesome to have you around again, just like old times."

Ivy smiled, blushing slightly. "I'll definitely think about it," she said. "Either way, I could always come in with Mom when she's working. We could hang out."

Whit grinned. "Good. I'll call you this weekend."

I exchanged a quick look with Ivy. He was going to call her!

"Great. You're here," Mrs. Scanlon said, appearing in the doorway. "Listen, Quincy's car is already downstairs waiting for you. I'll arrange for the hotel to hold our luggage in the lobby. You guys are going to need to go right now if you still want to see some sights."

"Okay, wait. You're going sightseeing with Quincy

Vanderstan?" Whit asked, shaking his head. "The stuff that happens to you four is mind-boggling. You really took *City Nation* by storm!"

"We seem to have that effect when the four of us get together," I said, laughing. "It was really great meeting you, Whit."

"Same here," he told me. "I think all four of you should come back. It's going to be incredibly boring here without you."

"Oh, we'll definitely come back!" Tally said. "I don't know how I can face school again now that I've been here!"

We all had our coats on, and Ivy's mom was gesturing for us to hurry.

"E-mail me when you're home and tell me how it went," Whit said to Ivy.

"Oh, I will," she told him. "I've got your new address."

A phone on one of the desks rang, and Whit quickly answered it.

"Intern room," he said, looking up and waving. Suddenly he was all business, and we left him to it.

"Well, I hope *City Nation* was everything you wanted it to be," Mrs. Scanlon said. "From what I hear, *4 Girls* made quite the splash."

"We had no idea it was going to be this great," I

said happily. "I don't think anybody will believe half the things that happened."

"They won't have to take your word for it," Mrs. Scanlon said. "They can see it for themselves online."

That's one of the best parts of the experience, I thought as I walked with my friends. It would all be there on our web issue so we could relive it again and again.

It was hard not to believe it was going to be the best *4 Girls* ever.

· chapter ·
14

I didn't know what was more unbelievable, the fact that we were sitting in an enormous limousine or that we were sitting in *Quincy Vanderstan's* limousine. I couldn't forget that she was a big star, and yet here we were sitting with her like she was a regular person.

"Everybody in? Let's go!" Quincy said.

The limo was huge. There were two seats facing each other, individual seats on one side along the door, and what looked like a miniature kitchen and entertainment system in the middle.

"You have to give me the address of your site so I can see it," Quincy told us, opening a laptop.

"Can you do that while we're driving?" I asked.

"You can do just about anything in this limo," Quincy said.

"Here—I'll do it," Miko said, and Quincy handed her the laptop.

"This is so great of you to show us some of the city," I said.

"Are you kidding? This is fun for me! And I owe you guys. You really helped me out yesterday. If I had stayed in that sample room any longer, Helvetica would have found out I went missing. I was such an idiot," Quincy said.

"Who doesn't get mad at their parents sometimes?" Miko asked. "We've all been there. That was a ton of pressure for you on that set."

"Did you get to talk to your mom about it at all?" Ivy asked.

"I did, actually," Quincy said. "She ended up being supernice about it. I think she was even more relieved than me that we got back on track without Helvetica finding out. Sometimes I forget that I'm not the only one whose life has turned upside down in the last year. She's pretty much made my career her full-time job."

"Oh, that reminds me of my question," I said. "Can I ask it now?"

"Shoot," Quincy said. "Ask me anything."

Miko tossed her camera to Ivy, who turned it on.

"Okay," I began. "So like you said, this has all happened really fast. You had the TV show last year, but then you got the movies, and it seemed like you suddenly skyrocketed to fame. What's changed the

161

most for you? And if you could get one thing back from your old life, what would it be?"

"Wow, that's a good question," Quincy said. "I can't even say what's changed the most because *everything* has changed. I was about to start my senior year in high school. We'd shot most of the show over the summer, but I had to have a tutor on set so we could keep on schedule. I never in a million years imagined myself saying this, but one thing I'd change back would be school. I really miss just being around people my own age, going through the regular old dramas, you know? Who's going to ask who to Spring Fling, who dropped their lunch in the cafeteria, who's trying out for the school play. It all seems kind of endless and boring when you're in it, but you can never get those days back. I really miss them."

I nodded thoughtfully.

"Can I ask my question now, too?" asked Tally.

"Sure," Quincy said.

"Well, I've wanted to be an actress since forever," Tally said. "My mother says I've been acting like the world is my stage since I learned to walk. I love acting, and I love going to the movies and to the theater, and I'm really sure it's what I want to do. And if someone offered me the chance to be famous like you, I wouldn't say no. I mean, who would?

But there must be things you don't like about being famous, on top of having to miss school," Tally said. "Is being an actress ever *less* fun when you become *more* famous?"

"Well, in terms of the acting itself, it's way more fun than ever," Quincy said. "I have so many more parts to choose from. There are so many options. I loved doing theater in school, and that's something I really want to get back to, but that's one of the downsides of being considered famous. You guys saw a little of what it was like yesterday on the shoot. There's a ton of people around, and if I lose my temper or have a bad moment, they all see it happen. It's hard to function when you're in the spotlight all the time. So as much as I really want to do a play, I kind of worry about it. What if I had a bad day in front of all those people? Would they think I was just being a diva, or would they tell stories about me to the press? What if the real me is so different than the celebrity me that people don't like me, or I disappoint them? Or what if I'm great for TV or film, where you can do stuff over again if you mess up, but I don't have what it takes to be a Broadway actress? Sometimes I think if I got a little less attention, I might feel more brave about trying new things. Does that make any sense?"

"It makes perfect sense," Tally said. "But you

shouldn't let that stop you from doing a play. You'd be a smash on Broadway. I know you would."

"Thanks," Quincy said. "And speaking of Broadway, check it out!"

We all looked out the window, and I took a deep breath as Tally exclaimed loudly.

"Oh, Times Square!" she cried.

We had driven down a street where all the buildings created this great opening—like a grand canyon in the center of the city. Every building seemed covered with brightly colored ads and pictures. On the side of one building was a massive television screen and above and below it were electronic billboards on which moving images flashed. I couldn't look at any one thing for too long because something else would catch my attention. My eyes went from a glassed-in television studio to a theater to a rotating, blinking Coca-Cola can to a store that seemed to sell nothing but M&Ms. There was so much to take in, and we were moving briskly with the traffic. There were so many people jammed onto the sidewalk, I was suddenly grateful to be in the quiet, roomy limousine. Times Square was overwhelming, but I wasn't sure I wanted to see it on foot, in the middle of all those people.

"I never get used to that sight," Ivy said. "Not even when I lived here. Times Square is always so crazy. That's why they call New York the 'city that never sleeps.'"

"You think it looks packed now—check it out tomorrow when the Thanksgiving parade comes through," Quincy remarked.

"Garamond said you're actually going to be in the parade," Miko said. "Is it true?"

Quincy nodded, grinning. "Yep! I'm way more nervous about that than the photo shoot. There's going to be thousands of people everywhere and millions watching on TV! What if I do something stupid? What if I have to, like, climb off my float and run into a Starbucks to use the bathroom?"

"Oh, but you're a star!" Tally exclaimed. "They should give you your own bathroom inside your float!"

Quincy laughed. "Maybe you should be my manager, Tally," she told her.

"Okay, so now that you've seen Times Square, we'll head somewhere a little quieter," Quincy explained. "Hey, guys, your site is really cool!"

"If you hit that link, it goes to the blog," Ivy pointed out. "You can see the comments people have been leaving about what we've put up so far."

"I want to see," Quincy said, pushing a button. "Oh wow. Here's a thread called 'Quincee'—they spelled my name wrong. Are all these comments about me?"

"Well, we didn't know who we were going to be interviewing until the day of the shoot," Ivy explained. "It turned into a big 'guess who it's going to be' thing."

"'Please tell Quincy Vanderstan she is my favorite actress,'" Quincy read. "Cool! 'Can you guys get Quincy to come to Bixby so we can meet her, too?' Hah—you never know. Oh, here's a good one: 'Ask Quincy what Johnny Depp is like in person.' Please. I wish I knew!"

"We get all different kinds of comments," I explained. "Some of them might seem silly. I'm sure nobody imagined you'd be reading them!"

"Want me to post a message?" Quincy asked, grinning.

"Wow, seriously? Would you do that?" Ivy asked. "Just a sentence or two. Everyone would go nuts!"

"Absolutely, let's do it," Quincy said.

"Here, I'll sign you in as Quincy Vanderstan," Miko said, turning the laptop toward her. "Okay, there you go."

We all watched as Quincy began to type, her tongue tucked in the corner of her mouth as she concentrated.

"Okay, how's this: Hi, *4 Girls* readers. Thanks for all the comments. I'm sitting here with Miko, Tally, Ivy, and Paulina having a great time in New York

City. This site is awesome, and I love reading your comments. I will definitely keep reading—I am *4 Girls'* biggest fan!"

"That's perfect! Everyone will love it!" I exclaimed.

"Can you leave my log-in so I can post again if I have time?" Quincy asked.

"Sure," Miko said, taking the laptop. "I'll just set a password for you. What do you want it to be?"

"Something I can't possibly forget," Quincy said.

"How about 'Helvetica'?" Ivy suggested.

Quincy laughed. "Perfect," she agreed.

Miko typed in the password. "All set," she said. "Oh wow—Ivy, look what your mom just e-mailed!"

Miko turned the computer so we could all see it. Mrs. Scanlon had sent the picture Raavi had taken of all of us at the photo shoot. I don't know how Raavi had managed it, but he seemed to have captured something utterly unique in each one of us. Quincy was giving a glamorous smile, but she had turned her head and arched one eyebrow like there was a secret we were all in on. Tally was grinning wildly, her eyes huge and clear, and her face flushed with all the excitement. Miko was standing up very straight with a cool, half smile, but I could see she was clutching Tally's arm very tightly. Ivy was looking slightly past the camera, around the spot where her mother had probably been standing. And I wasn't looking at the camera at all, I was looking at the four girls standing with me, and my face was just starting to go into a full smile. I actually looked like I was about to laugh.

It was amazing that one picture could say so much. Whatever the finished web issue contained, whatever footage and stories made it in, and whatever details never appeared, it was all contained in this one single image, what the four of us were individually, and what we became together in one glorious day.

•   •   •   •   •   •   •

Quincy tapped on the glass separating the back area from the front. "Hey, Tom, can you pull over for a minute so we can get out?"

The car came to a stop, and Quincy opened the door. "Come see!" she said.

We got out on the sidewalk, where the whole city seemed to be divided into two worlds.

"This is my favorite place in Manhattan," Quincy said. "Central Park."

On one side of the street were big buildings and on the other a paved path led into a world of grass and trees. The park seemed to go on forever. Near the entrance was a line of horse-drawn carriages. There were hot dog vendors and tables set up where you could buy anything from a purse to T-shirts. People were streaming into the park—joggers, mothers pushing strollers, and couples taking pictures or just walking and holding hands.

"It's beautiful," I exclaimed. "I wish we had time to walk through it."

"We can, if you want," Quincy said. "They might already be getting set up to start inflating some of the balloons for the parade. Or we can keep driving and see something else. I know you guys have a train to catch. Why don't you decide? Whatever you want, I'm game."

I had no idea where to go, but Tally seemed to be about to explode.

"I have a feeling Tally has a suggestion," Miko said.

"Oh I do, but we should all decide," Tally said, making a visible effort to control herself.

"Well, anything is fine with me," Ivy said. "I spent most of my life here. You guys pick."

Miko and I exchanged a look.

"What do you think, Miko? Are we okay with Tally picking our final stop in New York?"

"Definitely," Miko said. "I'm sure whatever it is, it will be dramatic."

• • • • • • •

After a blur of traffic, a short line, and an awe-inspiring elevator ride, I had to agree that Tally had made a perfect choice. It was nothing if not dramatic.

We were standing together on the observation deck of the most impressive building in Manhattan. We could see almost the entire island the city was built upon, with the East River running up one side, and the Hudson River on the other. To the south, the Statue of Liberty was clearly visible on its own tiny island and to the north the sun glinted off the top of the Chrysler Building, which glimmered like a jewel against the bright blue sky. The sight was absolutely breathtaking. I realized for the first time just how massive the city really was. It was busier and even more exciting than I'd imagined, and at the same time, it made me feel very small. And a little homesick. Soon it would be time to head to Grand Central to catch the train home. So much had happened in the last three days, I would be sorry to leave the city, but very glad to get home.

"I can't believe it! The Empire State Building!" Tally said for the twentieth time.

"Why don't you give me your camera, and I'll record the four of you saying good-bye from the city," Quincy suggested.

She had put on a baseball cap and sunglasses, and to my amazement none of the hundreds of people milling around us seemed to realize a movie star was in their midst.

"That would be great!" Miko said, giving Quincy her camera.

We all stood together near the railing.

"Talk loudly," Quincy said. "The sound will be hard to pick up because it's so windy up here."

"You start, Ivy," I suggested.

"Hi, readers! *4 Girls* here," Ivy began. "Well, our trip is just about over. We've had an amazing couple of days at *City Nation*."

"I hope our video and articles give you an idea of what it's like to work at a magazine," Tally said.

"It has been unbelievable seeing all the work it takes to bring just one issue to the readers," Miko added.

"I feel like we've seen it all, but I know we've really had only a tiny glimpse into what goes into publishing a big magazine," I added. "We had a blast, but we can't wait to get home!"

"Keep your questions and comments coming," Ivy said. "You never know who's going to be reading them."

Quincy turned the camera around to capture her own image.

"I know I will," she said. "These *4 Girls* rule!"

Then she panned the camera in a full circle to capture the people around us, the buildings looming up beyond them, and the horizon in the distance.

It was the perfect way to end our trip. A movie star was filming US. We were literally up in the clouds, and the world was spread at our feet. I for one felt like there was nothing we couldn't do. We had triumphed in New York City. And where would we take *4 Girls* next?

Well, that was up to us. The sky was the limit.

· chapter ·

15

"It's Spider-Man! Epic!" Kevin yelled, waving his plastic lightsaber wildly in the air, narrowly missing the coffee table, as the sight of a massive, airborne Spider-Man filled the television screen.

I ducked, and Ivy made a protective grab for her mug of steaming cocoa.

"Please excuse my demented brother," I said to Ivy. "He gets crazy around the holidays."

"You don't have to tell me that—I was here on Halloween, remember?" Ivy said, laughing. "Oh look—there's a shot of Times Square!"

I had watched the Macy's Thanksgiving Day Parade on television every year since I could remember. But seeing it now, when just the day before I'd been in New York City myself, was more exciting than ever. Times Square was jam-packed with parade-goers, and the sky was filled with massive, brightly colored balloons, but on television the sheer enormity of the place didn't fully come through. Now that I had been there, I felt like I was seeing the parade in a whole new way. I felt like part of it all now. I felt excited, and even a little more grown-up.

"Kevin, we were right in that exact place yesterday," I said, pointing to the television.

"Did you see Spider-Man? Did you see Sonic? Did you see Buzz Lightyear?" Kevin asked, issuing each question in rapid-fire succession.

"They weren't there yet," I told my little brother. "They inflated the balloons last night in Central Park. We did see Central Park itself, though."

"Why would anyone go all the way to New York City and not stay to see Spider-Man?" Kevin asked, shaking his head. "You're nuts."

"Maybe," I replied. "But I'm happy to be home and watching the parade on TV, instead of standing there with all those zillions of people."

My mother walked in from the kitchen, wiping her hands on a dish towel.

"Do you guys need anything?" she asked.

"It smells incredible in there," Ivy said. "I'm starting to wish I was having Thanksgiving at your house. My mom used to buy Thanksgiving dinner in the city—getting the turkey all cooked from Fairway Market and her pies already baked from Zabar's.

Doing it all by herself is a little more challenging than she thought. I was kind of glad to get out of the house this morning!"

"Hey, there she is—there's your famous friend!" Kevin shouted, pointing at the TV. "And check out the Dr. Wow float! Wow!"

We stopped talking to watch, and Ivy exclaimed excitedly, "Oh my gosh, yes! There she is—there's Quincy!"

The Dr. Wow float was a quirky reproduction of the little house that was actually a spaceship, where the characters on the show spent most of their time. It was a bright red, wooden structure that leaned slightly to one side and had a sharply peaked roof under which was one tiny window.

Quincy and the actor who played Dr. Wow were on a platform outside the house, both wearing their costumes. The float was escorted by a perky group of baton-twirling majorettes in bright green uniforms and knee-high white boots.

My cell phone began to ring. I glanced at the screen, and hit ANSWER and SPEAKER at the same time.

"Oh my gosh, are y'all watching this?" a voice shrieked from my phone. "Are y'all seeing the same thing I'm seeing?"

"Yes, it's Quincy on the Dr. Wow float!" I said. "Ivy's here, too."

"And Kevin!" yelled Kevin.

"Hey, everybody—can y'all believe it? We were in a limo with her one day ago!"

"We can believe it," Ivy said. "Because it really happened. And we have the pictures to prove it."

As the Dr. Wow float drove by the media stand, there was a close-up shot of Quincy standing and waving, her brilliant smile never wavering. As she came even with the camera she turned and looked at it, giving a half wave, with four fingers spread wide and her thumb tucked underneath. Still looking right into the camera, Quincy winked.

Tally's shriek came through my phone speaker loud and clear.

"Did you see that? She held up four fingers and winked. That was for us!" Tally yelled.

"Tal, I think she was just waving," I said as Ivy's phone began to buzz.

"Got a text from Miko," Ivy said. "It says, 'OMG, Quincy totes just gave us a shout-out.'"

"See?" squealed the tiny Tally voice. "Miko agrees!"

"It did sort of look like a message for you guys," my mom agreed. "Quincy's just beautiful, isn't she? I'm so glad to know she's a nice person in real life. What a story—you girls will be telling it for the rest of your lives!"

A buzzer went off in the kitchen, and my mother quickly headed back in that direction.

On the television, the Dr. Wow float had already passed by the cameras, and the crowd was now focusing on a giant SpongeBob gliding down the street.

"Has Miko said anything else about her parents?" I asked Ivy.

"Not much," Ivy said. "I pretty much heard the same thing she told you—she got home, told her parents about the design internship, and they went ballistic and told her she's going to the Music Conservatory for the summer and that's that."

I sighed. "Poor Miko," I said.

"Well, it's not the worst problem to have in the world," Ivy pointed out. "She's got two amazing summer opportunities, both for things she's really good at and could probably do professionally. The only hard thing is she has to choose one over the other. At least I'm guessing she'd have to choose. I don't know—maybe there's a way for her to do both—Garamond might be willing to be flexible."

"But how do you pick between two things like that?" Tally asked, startling me slightly. I'd forgotten she was still there on the phone.

"I don't know," Ivy replied. "We'll just have to watch and see how she handles it. And learn, hopefully. 'Cause sooner or later, we're all going to have to start making choices like that. Like, do we want to go to college? Maybe get a job to help pay for it? Do we want to try getting an internship over the summer, too? Or a summer overseas—maybe the Peace Corps? Or stay at home doing absolutely nothing every summer while we still can? There's a lot of choices, and high school isn't as far away as we'd like to think it is."

"I heard some girls near my locker say that exact same thing right before Thanksgiving break," I said. "Hey, maybe Miko would let us sort of follow her story for *4 Girls*—I mean not the part about arguing with her parents, obviously, but the other part. How she has these two great opportunities and pursuing one over the other would mean really different things for her life. What is she going to end up choosing? What will it be like?"

"Oh, it's so dramatic!" Tally breathed.

"I think it's a great idea," Ivy told me. "Let's wait until after break when things have had a chance to settle down for Miko a little, then ask her. I wonder which one she will end up doing."

"How important a decision is it, I wonder?" I asked. "I mean, if she picks the internship, does that mean she'll probably end up working as a designer? And if she picks the Music Conservatory, she'll end up a violinist? It could affect the outcome of her *entire* life. That's so much pressure."

"Miko can handle the pressure," Ivy said. "But you're right—the story of it—how it all unfolds and how it ends up—that would be an amazing article for the magazine."

A small scream came from my phone.

"What was that?" Ivy asked.

"My sister's beagle has got one of the pumpkin pies," Tally cried. "I was supposed to be watching him. I gotta go! Buddy, drop it. Drop it!"

"What?" Kevin asked, the sound of Tally's shriek temporarily diverting him from the sight of the parade.

"I think Tally's dog might have just eaten their dessert," I said, laughing.

"Bummer!" Kevin yelled. "We're having two pies, pumpkin and apple, and I'm having both!"

"Speaking of Thanksgiving meals, I should probably get going," Ivy said.

"Oh, okay," I said, standing up with Ivy. "I'm so glad we got to watch the parade together. Do you think Quincy was really winking at the four of us?"

"I think nobody can prove she wasn't," Ivy replied with a smile. "And it makes a great story. So are you still on with Benny tonight?"

I felt a slight flush come over my face.

"Yep," I said. "We're going to meet down at Strange Brew for some hot spiced cider."

"That is very romantic," Ivy said.

Kevin immediately began staggering around making throwing-up noises. I led Ivy out of the room and down the hallway toward the front door.

"So?" I asked my friend as we reached the door.

"So what?" she asked.

I nudged her. "So what about you? Have you heard from Whit?"

"You mean other than since we spoke on the phone last night and after he sent a good-night text, both of which I told you about?"

I nodded. "Yeah, other than that."

Ivy gave me a slow smile. "He did send a really short text this morning asking if I might be able to Skype after dinner."

I clapped my hands. "I knew it!" I exclaimed.

"You don't know anything, and neither do I," Ivy said. "We'll just have to wait and see what happens. I mean, it could go either way. Like with Miko."

"So you're leaving me with this cliff-hanger?" I teased. I mustered my best Dramatic Movie Announcer voice. "Will Miko Suzuki be the city's next design wizard or will she take the music world by storm? Will Ivy Scanlon and Whit Clayton finally start dating after meeting in kindergarten seven years ago, or will she leave him to Dakota's evil devices?"

"Will Paulina Barbosa be found locked in her own bedroom with a piece of duct tape over her mouth?" Ivy finished. "Coming to a theater near you soon: In a world where anything can happen, and usually does, travel to the crazy and the comic, the triumphant and the tragic, with a group of four girls thrown together in an innocent bid to publish a magazine. Little did they know they would end up . . . Forever Four! Cue sound track!"

"Perfect," I said, laughing. "Our own movie. I'd go see it."

"So would I," Ivy said. "I'm dying to find out how it's all going to turn out."

"Me too," I agreed. "Me too."

But for that, we were just going to have to be patient and wait for things to unfold.

And if the last few months were any indication, things would happen at lightning speed and bring a load of surprises along the way.

I couldn't wait to see what they were.

coming soon:

forever FOUR

· staying in tune ·

· chapter ·

1

I felt a ripple of excitement as the auditorium lights dimmed and Miko Suzuki walked confidently onto the stage, her violin in one hand. In the seat next to me, Tally Janeway was nervously wiggling her foot. At the sight of our friend, Tally's foot wiggling doubled in speed and intensity. On my other side, my best friend, Ivy Scanlon, was watching Miko intently, her pale-blue eyes shining with anticipation. I took a deep breath as a white-haired woman followed Miko onstage and sat down at a grand piano. The audience fell completely silent.

I felt as excited as Ivy looked and as nervous as Tally's jiggling foot indicated she was. The four of us had been spending a lot of time with each other since coming together to create *4 Girls* magazine back in September. Though I'd always known Miko was superserious about playing the violin, I'd never actually heard her play. That was all about to change.

Miko looked gorgeous in a red velvet dress with a black flower sewn on the left shoulder. Her glossy black hair was pulled back from her face with shiny silver clips. Miko always looked great, but tonight there was something different. Something WONDERFUL. She seemed to fill the entire stage with her presence. *Maybe that's what confidence looks like*, I thought.

Tucking her violin under her chin, Miko raised the bow over the strings, her eyes trained on the pianist. The woman at the piano gave a small nod and played a few notes on the keys. Then it was all Miko.

My mouth dropped open slightly as Miko pulled the bow back and forth across the strings, and the most AMAZING sound filled the auditorium. One part whine, one part soul, and a whole lot of emotion came through in just a few notes. I'd never listened to a violin solo before, but now I would try to pick that heartfelt sound out of every orchestral ensemble I heard for the rest of my life. Next to me, I heard Tally give a quiet sigh. The song was sweet and nostalgic. I'd listened to the short tune, called "Salut d'Amour," on my iPod a few times after Miko had told me it was one of the pieces she would be playing. But as I watched my friend play the familiar notes with her own hands, I felt my breath catch in my throat. There was a brief silence as Miko finished the song and lowered her violin.

Then the auditorium filled with the sound of applause.

"I knew she was good, but I had no idea she was *that* good," Ivy exclaimed.

"Right?" I said, clapping loudly. "She played it perfectly. Now she plays the second piece—the one by Bach."

Miko stood still, acknowledging the audience with a small smile. I stopped clapping and clasped my hands tightly in my lap. I had asked Miko incessantly about proper behavior at a classical music concert. I'd heard that there were certain times when you were supposed to clap politely and other times you were supposed to wait until the conductor or musician nodded slightly. Miko had explained that if you were listening to a long piece, like a sonata or symphony, you shouldn't applaud during the brief pauses between movements, but it was okay to clap for a few moments after one piece ended and before a new one began.

When Miko raised the violin to her chin again, everyone fell silent. I knew this piece, called "Ave Maria." I hummed along silently inside my head as Miko played the familiar tune. Her eyes were closed slightly, and her brow was furrowed in concentration.

Miko's right hand, carefully holding her bow over the strings, looked both strong and graceful. The song ended with a long, low note.

Miko opened her eyes, lowered her violin again, and took a bow. I began to clap wildly.

"Bravo!" Tally was calling. "Encore!"

"Yes, encore!" I cried, echoing Tally, but the applause was so loud I'm sure Miko couldn't hear us all the way up on the stage.

Miko gave another bow, then gestured toward the pianist, who stood and took a bow, too. Then Miko walked offstage, extremely graceful in heels so high I probably could not even stand still in them without tottering.

There were two other performers in the program. One was a boy around Miko's age, and one was a girl several years older. They both played pieces by Mozart. If I had only come to hear the two of them, I would have been impressed that they could play at all. But following Miko's performance, I could hear subtle mistakes in each of their songs when they weren't quite in tune. *Miko has really got something special*, I thought as the lights came up in the auditorium. I followed Ivy and Tally to the lobby, superexcited to see our friend and applaud her performance in person.

"Can you guys believe how good she was?" I

exclaimed. "I'm a little nervous to see her right now."

"Ivy, text her again!" Tally said impatiently. I took the small bouquet of flowers we'd all pitched in to get from Tally, afraid she'd crush them in her excited grip. "What if she goes out the stage door and we don't see her?"

Ivy laughed. "Tal, this isn't Carnegie Hall," she said. "She'll come out the same door as everyone else. Besides, her parents are standing right over there. You think she's going to leave without them?"

"Ooh, guys, I see her!" I said.

Miko had come into the lobby and headed straight for her parents. Her mother gave her a big hug, and her father began talking and waving his hands around while Miko nodded.

"The transitions have to be crisper in Bach, Miko," he was saying. "There's a difference between holding back and just sounding like you don't know the piece you are playing."

Whoa. I wondered what performance Miko's dad had seen, because I was pretty sure it wasn't the same one *I'd* seen. Miko had sounded spectacular to me.

"And you have to make that legato smoother while still leaving a break between the two notes," he continued. "We've talked about this before."

Miko was looking at the floor, chewing her lower lip and nodding.

"But your bowing was perfect and you played with such sensitivity, Miko," her mother said. "I love it when you play like that—so sophisticated, and I can hear the emotion in the piece. Smoothing out those transitions will be easy for you to fix."

"Thanks, Mom," Miko said.

"Yes, that aspect was excellent. But back to the issue of contrasts, Miko," her father continued. Then he leaned in closer, and I couldn't hear what he was saying any longer.

Miko caught my eye for a fraction of a second, still nodding as she listened to her father. When he paused to take a breath, Miko pointed. Her mother turned, and when she spotted us across the room, she waved and gave Miko a little nudge. Miko rushed over to where we were waiting.

"You guys are so great to come to my recital," Miko said.

I laughed. "Of course we would come," I told her. "You've been working toward this for so long. You blew us away up there!"

"That music was *sooo* romantic," Tally declared. "Especially the first song. What was it again?"

"Elgar's 'Salut d'Amour,'" Miko said.

"It is actually a love song," I said. "Elgar wrote it as an engagement present for his fiancée."

"Wow, Paulie, you've really done your homework," Miko said, looking impressed.

Tally drew in a deep breath and clasped her hands together in front of her heart. "Oh, wouldn't you just die if someone wrote a song like that for you? I would cry every time I heard it for the rest of my life, no matter how old I got to be. And if I couldn't hear the song, I would just say the name over and over again. Salut d'Amour. Salut d'Amour. Salut d'Amour."

"These are for you—from all three of us," I said, handing Miko the bouquet of bright red roses.

"They're beautiful," Miko said warmly. "I love them. Thank you so much!" She smiled at us, then glanced around the room for a moment, like she was looking for someone else.

"You deserve them, Miko, really. You sounded like a pro," Ivy said.

Miko looked embarrassed. "Oh, guys. Come on. It's not *that* hard of a piece. I did get through it with no mistakes, but my dad's right, it was still far from perfect."

"It sounded perfect to *me*," I said. "Both pieces did. And you played them without reading the music! It must have taken you forever to learn them by heart."

Miko laughed. "Oh, you'd be amazed," she said. "Forever is more like three weeks. A professional violinist could learn those songs in a day or two, though. Seriously, guys, I'm a long way from the big leagues, according to my dad."

"Don't be so humble," I said, giving Miko a nudge. "We've personally witnessed you wowing the big leagues, remember?"

"Speaking of which, any news on the internship?" Ivy asked. "Have you talked to Garamond again?"

Ivy's mother had arranged for us to go to New York City to do a special web edition of our magazine from inside one of the most famous magazines around: *City Nation*. Miko had impressed Garamond, the managing editor, and the entire design department with her keen eye for style. Garamond had encouraged her to apply for one of the coveted summer internships and even offered to help her get her application just right.

"It's looking pretty impossible at this point," Miko said. "My dad saw the application Garamond sent and kind of went ballistic. He said the city is too far to commute every day, and if I was staying there one of my parents would have to stay, too. I mean, I'd love to do it—it would be like a dream come true. But Dad is really pushing for the Music Conservatory program, which would be a different kind of amazing. I wish I could do them both. But since the Music Conservatory is much closer to home, I think I'm going to have to tell Garamond that I just can't apply for the *City Nation* internship."

I looked at Miko carefully. Something didn't seem right—Miko never backed down from a challenge. At least not before she had all the answers in front of her. If she didn't *get* the *City Nation* internship, then she could still focus on the Music Conservatory. But to not even try? I was starting to wonder just how much Miko's father was influencing her choices.

"Did you already get accepted to the conservatory?" Tally asked.

"Not yet," Miko said. "I submitted the application. The music audition and written tests are in a couple weeks. I'm going to have to practice every spare minute I have from now until then, and my dad got me a music coach to study theory and prepare for the written exam. I was hoping to create another original cover for the next *4 Girls* issue, but I'm not going to have time. Again! I'm so sorry."

"You have nothing to be sorry about," I assured her. "We'll just do what we did before. You'll help when you can, and we'll get it all done. We don't even need the next issue completed for another two and a half weeks. That's the great thing about making it a winter issue instead of a December issue—we ended up with some extra time!"

"And with all the requests we've had on the blog for people to be able to contribute, we're thinking the whole theme is going to be kind of like a collaboration between *4 Girls* and our readers. All the contributions would mean less writing for us to do this time around," Ivy chimed in.

"Okay, good," Miko said, looking relieved. "I'm totally on board with helping out and going to meetings when I can. I told my parents that *4 Girls* is as much a priority for me as this conservatory audition is for them."

"Speaking of your parents, here comes your mom," Ivy said.

Miko's mother was a petite, elegant-looking woman in a deep-blue pantsuit, her graying hair pulled up in a bun.

"Hi, Mrs. Suzuki," I said.

"Hi, girls," Mrs. Suzuki said. "Tally, Ivy, Paulina, it's so nice to see you here supporting Miko. Thank you for coming."

"We wouldn't have missed it for the world," I said. "We haven't seen enough of Miko lately. She's been so busy. But guess what, Meek—my mom says I can have some friends over on New Year's. Can you come?"

Miko looked quickly at her mother, but Mrs. Suzuki was already shaking her head.

"That's very nice of you," Mrs. Suzuki said. "But a friend of Miko's dad's will be visiting us that night, and he is a very successful pianist. He thinks it would be helpful for Miko to talk to him about her audition."

"On New Year's Eve?" Miko said. "Was Dad even going to ask me about this, or is it all decided?"

"I thought he had, Miko," Mrs. Suzuki said. "He thought you'd be excited about it."

Miko said nothing, but turned slightly away from her mother and rolled her eyes a little.

"Sorry," Miko told me. "I would have loved to have come. I guess the three of you will have to ring in the new year without me."

"Oh, I can't go, either," Tally said. "The whole Drama Club is going to Buster's cousin's house. His parents are pastry chefs! We're going to eat like kings and queens! Tea cakes and petits fours and meringues and raspberry cheesecake tarts!"

"Are you serious? Can you get some for us?" Miko asked. "My favorite dessert in the world is—"

"Sweetheart, your father is waiting," Mrs. Suzuki said. "We're supposed to get coffee with your teacher to talk about your performance, remember?"

I could see Miko's father looking impatient. He kept glancing at his watch. *Poor Miko*, I thought. *Why can't he let her enjoy being with her friends for just five minutes?*

Miko sighed softly. "I'd better go. You guys,

seriously, thanks so much for coming. It means . . . a lot."

"An alien invasion could not have kept me away," Tally declared. "Actually, I wouldn't be surprised if we ran into an alien invasion on the way home. I saw this TV show about this race of space people that are hypnotized by the sounds of string instruments—it's like some kind of communication or something for them, and if they happen to be passing close enough to a concert they steer the spaceship straight for—"

"Tal, she's gotta go," I said. Tally's stories could go on all night long, and Miko was out of time.

Miko's mother walked toward Mr. Suzuki, making a little "hurry up" gesture to Miko. Miko quickly scanned the room like she was hoping to see somebody else in the crowd.

"Thanks again for coming, you guys," Miko said. She gave us each a quick hug. "And if I don't talk to you before, have a great New Year's! Can you believe we only have three more days until school starts again?"

"I can't believe it," I said. "It seems like we just went on break. See you later, Miko. And great job, again."

As Miko rejoined her parents, my phone beeped and I checked the screen.

I'm outside. Are you ready to go?

"Hey, guys, my mom's waiting for us," I said.

Tally zipped her coat—a massive, ankle-length down jacket that she completely disappeared into. I had learned many things about Tally Janeway, future famous actress, and one of them was that she simply could not stand to be cold.

"I'm ready," Ivy said. She had on a simple navy-blue wool coat and a blue-and-white-striped scarf. If Tally was the picture of extravagance, Ivy was the exact opposite. Simplicity was her style.

"One second," Tally said, fumbling in her enormous purse and pulling out two fat mittens, a scarf, and a purple-and-green wool hat with two long, hanging strings that made it look like the hat had pigtails.

Ivy tried to hide the small smile pulling at her lips as Tally pulled the hat over her mass of wild blond curls and yanked it down as far it would go without covering her eyes.

"I did say my mom was right outside," I told Tally. "We don't have far to walk. And the car will be heated."

"Your version of heat is different than *my* version of heat," Tally insisted. "The weather report this morning said it was going to be thirty below zero today!"

"Um, I believe the actual report said thirty degrees," Ivy corrected her. "When they don't specify, they mean *above* zero."

"It's like the South Pole out there," Tally said. "It sure feels like thirty *below*."

Tally sighed and looked ruefully toward the exit, like a polar explorer about to leave her hut and trudge toward the South Pole. "Okay, I'm ready," Tally said, her voice slightly muffled since her chin and lips were covered by the collar of her coat.

"Are you absolutely sure?" Ivy asked playfully. "I can still see your nose."

Tally wrapped her scarf around her head so that only her eyes were visible above it. Then she nodded.

As we headed out the door, I caught my breath as a blast of wind hit me. It *was* pretty cold out! But, as promised, my mother was waiting in a warm car right outside the concert hall with my little brother, Kevin, in the front seat.

As me, Tally, and Ivy squished into the backseat, it hit me how sad I was that Miko wasn't with us. I was superexcited for her about the concert and the audition for the conservatory, but at the same time I felt bad. I'd always known Miko's dad had put a huge amount of pressure on her to be perfect. But with this audition coming up, I had a feeling Miko was going to be even more stressed out from the pressure at home. And knowing her parents, they weren't going to let her spend much time on anything else. Including us.

ABOUT THE AUTHOR

Elizabeth Cody Kimmel is a widely published author of thirty books for children and young adults, including *The Reinvention of Moxie Roosevelt* and the *Suddenly Supernatural* and *Lily B.* series. Elizabeth is proud to admit that she was never asked to sit at the Prom-Queens-in-Training table in her middle-school cafeteria. She likes reading, hiking, peanut butter cups, and *Star Trek*, but not at the same time. You can visit her at www.codykimmel.com.